What Ya Girl Won't Do

What Ya Girl Won't Do

Brandi Johnson

www.urbanbooks.net

Urban Books, LLC
300 Farmingdale Road, NY-Route 109
Farmingdale, NY 11735

What Ya Girl Won't Do
Copyright © 2013 Brandi Johnson

ISBN 13: 978-1-60162-03-6
ISBN 10: 1-60162-903-6

First Mass Market Printing April 2019
First Trade Paperback Printing August 2013
Printed in the United States of America

10 9 8 7 6 5 4 3 2 1

*This is a work of fiction. Any references or similar-
ities to actual events, real people, living or dead,
or to real locales are intended to give the novel a
sense of reality. Any similarity in other names,
characters, places, and incidents is entirely coin-
cidental.*

Distributed by Kensington Publishing Corp.
Submit Orders to:
Customer Service
400 Hahn Road
Westminster, MD 21157-4627
Phone: 1-800-733-3000
Fax: 1-800-659-2436

In Memory of my Daddy

Charles Woodruff

Gone but NEVER FORGOTTEN
07/07/1941–04/12/2013

Acknowledgments

As always I want to thank God for allowing me to press forward and finish this book during some trying times in my life. I didn't think I could do it, but He showed up in the midst of my storm, wrapped His arms around me and said YES YOU CAN . . . Thank You God for not allowing me to give up!

I have to give a shout out to my three heartbeats. . . . Montias, Brei'yonte and Amir'aki . . . you guys always seem to put a smile on mommy's face no matter what . . . God knew what He was doing when He blessed me with you three . . . You guys are my EVERYTHING. . . . I love y'all . . .

To my mommy . . . the only words that come to mind right now are Thank you and I love you for allowing me to be me. . . .

To my sister from another mother A.K.A. my "hip bone", you are the voice behind my fingers . . . Thank you for putting it down for me for the 5th time . . . Words can't explain how grateful I am to have you as my friend . . . You already know I value and appreciate all that you do for me . . .

Joylynn Jossel-Ross, I have to say you have gone above and beyond being my agent. Thank you for giving me that extra push when I tried to throw the towel in. Thank you for making me realize that I can rumble wit' some of the best authors in the literary game, thank you for believing in. . . .

Hugs and Kisses to all my brothers and sisters . . . No matter how much we fuss and fight please know and remember I love y'all with all my heart and it feels good knowing my big brothers and sisters will always believe in me.

Big ups to my newfound brothers . . . Shawn "Rude Boy" Ramsey, Darnell "Mike Jones" Jones, Julio "Ju" Taylor and last but not least, Joel "Scrumptious" Jackson . . . thank you guys for always having my back and being here for me especially when I needed a good laugh. Stay focused and always remember 4 1 4 The Po' 1 4 Life. . . .

To my niece Jaz'Mire Jackson I really need you to know that all the hard work you put in for me is not done in vain. And always remember that I love you and will drown a fish over you. . . .

To my god daughter Jamila Cobb keep ya' head up and don't let nobody steal ya' shine!!! Keep smilin' cuz' God has something good in store for you...

To my girl Tysha Hill . . . thanks for all the advice . . . You and I have been doing this a long time . . . It's our turn to show up and show out!!!!

I have to give a big shout out to my "Sleepover Crew" . . . You ladies put a smile on my face at times when I thought it was impossible to do with the battle rapping (which I am the Queen at) the Karaoke (sorry for always hogging the mic) and the "One Mo" shot (which I'm always game to take) Thanks for making the sleepovers fun!!!!

To Tammy Macklin and Patty (Peggy) Brooks I want to thank you ladies for having my back as well . . . You two are my biggest supporters and I love y'all for that . . .

R.I.P Al-Rahman A. Allah . . . A.K.A . . . Joe Louis . . . I love you!!!!!

They say you supposed to always save the best for last. . . . So I want to give a special shout out to all my readers . . . It's because of YOU I continue on my literary journey . . . thanks for your support . . . much love!!!!

Chapter One

Kylee lay alongside the pool of a million-dollar home of one of her many male friends, looking like one of America's Next Top Models while soaking up the hot sun. She smiled as she watched Tony jump off the diving board, making a huge splash.

"Bravo," she cheered loudly when he came up for air.

"You liked that?" Tony asked, smiling as he struggled to climb out of the pool.

"Yes, that was nice," Kylee answered with an exaggerated smile as Tony made his way over to her. The sight of him with his shirt off had her feeling a little disgusted. His greasy hair, big round, hairy belly, and jacked-up teeth were not an appealing sight.

"I see it don't take much to impress you," he joked, leaning down to give her a kiss.

"Hold on," Kylee said, throwing her hands up to stop Tony.

"What's the matter?" he asked, puzzled.

"You drippin' water all over my lace-front. And this here," she said, pointing to her hair, "was not cheap!"

"I'm sure I'm the one who paid for it, like I pay for everything else, so I'm allowed to get it wet." Tony closed his eyes, threw his head back, and let out a hearty laugh.

Kylee grimaced as she watched Tony's big, round belly jiggling in front of her face. *You wish you were the only one payin' for everything,* she thought as Tony bent down to kiss her.

"Excuse me, sir," Marta, the maid, interrupted right before Tony's lips met with Kylee's.

Tony stood upright and shot Marta a "this better be important" look. "Yes, Marta?" he answered with an attitude.

By the look on her boss's face, Marta didn't know if she should continue.

Kylee was relieved that Marta had interrupted them. The last thing she wanted to do was lock lips with this fat, greasy-head mob boss whose breath always reeked of fresh ass: hers, his wife's, and she was quite sure several others for free.

Marta looked at Kylee for a brief second before turning her attention back to Tony. "Mrs. Sparacio is due home in less than an hour, sir," she spoke in a heavy Spanish accent.

Tony looked at his watch. "Oh wow, how time flies when you're having fun. It's been two weeks already?" he said aloud.

"Yes, sir," Marta answered with a nod.

Hearing that, Kylee had no time to play. She needed to act quickly, especially if her plan for extra funds was going to work. "What if I told you I'm not ready to leave?" she looked up at Tony and asked, as she lifted her white Alexander Wang cat-eye sunglasses from her face.

"Awww, darlin', I know you don't wanna leave ol' Tony, but the missus is on her way home from Italy."

"I thought we was goin' out of town today to do some shoppin'," Kylee pouted as she stood up from the lounging chair.

The look on Kylee's face tore Tony up. He hated disappointing his black nigger bitch with the bangin' body and great head game, as he referred to her to some of his colleagues. He grabbed Kylee by the waist and pulled her close to him. She quickly held her breath before he started talking, not wanting to be exposed to the foul smell. "We were, but that was before my wife was due back. Marta, go get my wallet," he demanded, knowing money always put a smile on all his women's faces, especially the black ones.

"Yes, sir," Marta said with a nod, before turning to walk away.

"So how much do I get?" Kylee inquired before holding her breath again before Tony had time to answer.

"How much do you want?"

Kylee thought of all the extra work she had put in this weekend sexually—being in a sixty-nine position sucking on Tony's small penis while he rammed blunt objects up in her va-jay-jay, on top of having to stick her finger inside his butthole in order for him to cum—and quickly came up with a number that she thought was feasible. "Well, I would like my monthly allowance doubled," she responded coyly, hoping he'd agree to it.

"If that's what it's gon' take to cheer my li'l chocolate drop up, then that's what it'll be," he said, lifting her chin with his finger.

"Thanks, big daddy." Kylee smiled widely as she waited impatiently for Marta to get back with Tony's wallet so she could get out of there.

"I like it when you call me daddy." Tony winked with a smile.

"Does it turn you on?" Kylee asked seductively.

"Here you go, sir," Marta said, handing Tony his wallet, interrupting him again before he had time to answer Kylee's question.

Kylee eyed the overly stuffed wallet. She could barely contain herself as she watched Tony count out twenty crisp one-hundred dollar bills. "Here you go, my chocolate pudding cup." He smiled, handing her the money.

"Thank you." Kylee snatched the money from Tony's hand, gave him a quick peck on the cheek, and grabbed her purse off the patio table before turning to walk away.

"Heyyy, I just gave you two thousand dollars and all I get is a measly peck on the cheek?" Tony questioned, feeling slightly disrespected.

"Oh, I'm sorry. It's just that your wife is on her way so I was just tryin'a get outta here before she gets home," Kylee lied, placing her money inside her purse before throwing the strap over her shoulder. She didn't have the courage to hurt the man's feelings that helped contribute to her lavish lifestyle. She couldn't let him know she couldn't stand kissing and having sex with him. She really couldn't let him know if it weren't for the $1,000-a-month allowance she got paid for doing that, she wouldn't think twice about him.

"Oh, okay. I thought you were tryin'a play ol' Tony for a fool or something," he said.

"Now, why would I do that, big daddy? You're way too good to me," Kylee said, rubbing his hairy chest, hoping to smooth things over.

Tony smiled. "Well give big daddy a kiss before you go then," he said, closing his eyes and puckering his lips.

As much as she wanted to say hell no, she'd been tortured enough to last her a lifetime, she knew to keep getting paid she had to suck it up and do what he asked. Kylee closed her eyes as well and leaned in. She was okay with the kiss at first until Tony's tongue and foul breath entered her mouth. She instantly got grossed out, but stuck it out. Kylee figured for $2,000, she'd kiss a wild dog.

"Okay, big daddy, I gotta go," Kylee said, quickly ending the kiss.

"Okay, I'll see you in a couple weeks, right?"

You think I would pass up a thousand dollars for fuckin' yo' fat ass? "Mos def," Kylee responded with a smile.

"Marta, show our guest out," Tony said before picking up a Cuban cigar and a lighter from the patio table.

"I'm fine, Marta. I know my way," Kylee said, grabbing her keys out of her purse and quickly making her way through the big mansion and out to one of her many graduation presents her daddy had gotten her.

Kylee opened the door to her brand-new Acura ZDX and hopped in all while trying to rub the skin off her lips. She leaned over, grabbed her cell phone out of the glove compartment, and began dialing. She buckled up her seat belt and peeled out of the horseshoe driveway like Speed Racer. She weaved in and out of traffic, trying her best to get to the mall, but not before stopping to scoop up her best friend, Ja'Nay.

Chapter Two

"Why do you continue to sleep wit' Tony if he grosses you out so much?" Ja'Nay asked as they pulled into the mall parking lot.

"Because he help keep a sista fly and pays my bills so I don't have to go out and work like my parents want me to, that's why," Kylee answered as she put the car in park. "What other reason could it be?"

"And so does Anthony, Ricco, Joshua, Cedric, Vaughn, Antoine, and Mario. Am I missin' anybody?" Ja'Nay asked sarcastically.

"Nope, I think you got 'em all," Kylee said, pulling down the visor to check her makeup before looking over at her friend. "You ready?"

"I'reon would be devasted if she found out you were sleepin' wit' her dad," Ja'Nay said.

"That's why I'reon doesn't know and betta not find out," Kylee warned.

"I guess," Ja'Nay said, opening the car door and getting out.

"I need a new purse, some shoes, and some more perfume," Kylee rambled as they walked into the mall.

"Aren't you afraid of these guys finding out that all you really care about is their money?" Ja'Nay questioned.

Here we go again, Kylee thought while rolling her eyes. "We still talkin' about me and the men who help take care of me? I thought we finished that conversation in the car," Kylee said before walking into the Vanity clothing store. "How many times are you gon' bring this up? These men should already know, and if they don't, shame on them."

"It's just that I be so worried about you sometimes," Ja'Nay replied sincerely.

"Worried about what?" Kylee asked before picking up a shirt from the rack and laying it up against Ja'Nay's chest to see how it would look on her.

"Worried about one of them niggas flippin' out on you one day," Ja'Nay answered.

"Girl, please." Kylee laughed. "I told you them niggas ain't gon' do shit to me but keep a sista laced." Kylee shook her head no before placing the shirt back on the rack.

"I mean take Tony for instance. He's a mob boss. A fuckin' mob boss," Ja'Nay repeated as if

Kylee didn't hear her the first time. "Don't you think if he found out you pretendin' to like him that one day he'll do somethin' to you or have somethin' done to you?"

Kylee knew her best friend was always worrying about something and had been that way since they were little girls. They had been thick as thieves since third grade when they'd both decided to put glue on the chair of the classroom tattletale. They'd bonded during their week of after school detention. They'd had each other's back since and shared everything except men. Over the years, Ja'Nay's home life had become a mess due to her parents' constant arguing and fighting. Ja'Nay would stay at Kylee's house for days at a time and her parents were so caught up in hating each other, they'd never even noticed she was gone. Ja'Nay loved being around Kylee's parents and watching how much in love they appeared to be. Even more so, Ja'Nay loved pretending this was her family, which was easy to do because Kylee's parents never treated her any differently. By the girls' freshman year of high school, Ja'Nay's parents had divorced. Ja'Nay and her mother kept the house and her father moved out, never looking back. While Ja'Nay's mom tried to make ends meet by working double shifts, Ja'Nay was either stuck at home alone or at Kylee's, which was fine with her.

"Worst-case scenario, you guys might find me swimmin' wit' the fishes," Kylee said jokingly.

"Kylee!" Ja'Nay squealed. "That shit ain't funny. I'm serious."

"Calm down, Nay-Nay." Kylee laughed as she continued searching for a shirt for her best friend. "And, besides, Tony is my dad's business partner and one of his best friends. And do you think he would actually hurt his goddaughter?"

Ja'Nay shrugged her shoulders. "I hope not."

"Girl, stop worryin'. I got this, okay?"

"I'll try," Ja'Nay replied, knowing it would be hard to do so.

"Now, can we finish shoppin' without you bringin' up my boy toys?" Kylee asked before continuing her search for more shirts.

"You know it's a shame that every man you mess with either has a wife or a girlfriend," Ja'Nay said abruptly, ignoring Kylee's request.

"And? I wouldn't have it any other way. You know I don't like messing with single men; they expect too much from you!"

"Like what?" Ja'Nay inquired.

"I wanna man who has to go home to his chick at night. I don't have time for no nigga tryin'a be up under me all night. A lot of single men be thinkin' it's more to y'all's relationship than what it really is," Kylee said before picking up two shirts for herself that she'd fallen in love with.

"I guess," Ja'Nay halfheartedly agreed.

"And they be tryin'a control you and shit," Kylee continued with a frown. "Tryin'a tell you what you can and can't do. Or where you can and can't go or, better yet, *who* you can and can't do!"

"You silly." Ja'Nay laughed.

"No, I'm serious. That's why from the gate I let a nigga know, all we doin' is fuckin', you gon' pay or buy me stuff with no strings attached and that's that! And they all agree so I don't see what the big deal is."

"Yeah, but what about their wives and girl-friends?"

"What about 'em?" Kylee asked with an uncaring attitude. "If they wanna help take care of me, then they can. If not, they need to stay the fuck out my lane and let me do me!"

"I just hate niggas who cheat, that's all," Ja'Nay said, shaking her head in disgust.

"I do too, but only the ones who cheat on me. I don't give a damn what they do to anybody else and I don't know why you care so much," Kylee said, walking over to a rack of purses. "All men cheat; even the ones you think don't, trust me, they do!"

Ja'Nay disagreed with her friend's last comment. There was no way Kylee was going to convince her that after twenty-four years of marriage her father had ever cheated on her mother. They had the perfect relationship, one she wished her own mother and father had before they'd gotten divorced.

"It's not that I care, but put yourself in their shoes," Ja'Nay suggested.

"I don't wanna put myself in their shoes, 'cause I rock red bottoms and them hoes wear Payless. You feel me?" she asked rhetorically.

Ja'Nay shook her head. She didn't know what had transpired in her best friend's life to make her think and act the way she did. She didn't know if it stemmed from getting everything handed to her on a platter by her father, or the numerous men she ran through who always let her have her way with them. Whatever it was, she sure needed to change her way of thinking and living.

"I don't give a fuck about them hoes for real!" Kylee said in a raised tone.

"Shhh, calm down," Ja'Nay said, slightly embarrassed as her best friend caught the attention of some of the other shoppers.

"Calm down my ass! You act like it's my fault these men cheat on their women. It's not my fault, it's their own," Kylee said angrily.

"How you figure that?" Ja'Nay argued, starting to get upset about the bullshit that had just spilled from her best friend's mouth.

"Well, if yo' bitch learn how to satisfy you, there would be no need to fuck wit' a bitch like me," Kylee said, pointing to herself. "You see I'm the bitch them niggas come to because I'm that chick who does what ya girl won't do and get paid swell for doing it!"

"That ain't nothin' to brag about." Ja'Nay frowned.

"I'm not braggin' about bein' that bitch. I'm just keepin' it real!" Kylee stated proudly.

"Don't you wanna settle down, fall in love, and have a family one day?" Ja'Nay asked.

"Fall in love? Settle down? Have a family? Fuck that! I'm content doin' me!"

"I guess, man," Ja'Nay said, feeling like no matter how many years she'd been trying to get through to her friend, there was no use.

"And as long as I'm not fuckin' yo' man—which you would never have to worry about 'cause I can't stand Quann—why should you care about them hoes and their feelin's? Fuck them hoes and their feelin's," Kylee snapped.

Ja'Nay shook her head again and sighed.

"Now, can we finish shoppin'?" Kylee asked, smiling.

"Yes, but I have one more question before we do." Ja'Nay smiled too.

"Oh my goodness, what now?" Kylee said, exasperated.

"Are you payin' for my stuff too?" Ja'Nay laughed.

"Girl, you know I got'chu." Kylee laughed too, as she and Ja'Nay made their way up to the register with all their expensive items being paid for just the way Kylee preferred . . . with someone else's money.

Chapter Three

Kylee was in the living room bumping DJ Khaled's "Take it to the Head" while working out in front of the TV when her cell phone began to ring. She grabbed the towel off the arm of the chair, and wiped her face before grabbing the remote and turning the music down. Kylee walked over to the end table to retrieve her ringing phone. She looked at the caller ID and rolled her eyes before picking the phone up from the charging dock.

"Hello," she answered, out of breath.

"What are you doing?" her father asked skeptically.

"Workin' out, Dad," Kylee answered, slightly annoyed because of her father's insinuation.

"Oh, well how come I haven't seen my only child's face in almost a week?" her father started in. "I told your mother it wasn't a good idea for us to get you your own place because we would never see you."

"I've been busy, Dad," Kylee said, stretching the truth.

"Busy doing what? Too busy to come over and to see your parents? Remember you only have one mother and one father. Once we're gone, you don't get another pair," her father said.

Kylee rolled her eyes into the top of her head. If she had a dollar for each time her father said those words to her, there would be no need to sleep with men for money.

"I've been busy lookin' for a summer job so I can help pay for some of the things I'll need for college this fall," Kylee lied again. Truth be told, she was busy juggling her time between men.

The thought of his only child going to college put a smile on her father's face, but at the same time having her way across the country had him feeling some kind of way. "Now you know your mother and I are only making you work to teach you some kind of responsibility," her father explained. "You've had a free ride your entire life and now that you're grown, we don't want you to think you can get everything handed to you without you having to work for it, you understand?"

"Yes, Daddy, I understand," Kylee answered, just to appease her father, knowing she'd always gotten and still could get anything she wanted from him and any other man she dealt with, with little to no work at all.

"Good."

"Well, Daddy, I need to finish workin' out. I need to stay in the habit in order to avoid the freshman fifteen," Kylee said, rushing her father off the phone before he steered their conversation to why she felt the need to go way to California just to go to college when they have hundreds of colleges in and around Ohio.

"Okay. Oh, before I forget, your godfather is having a cookout this weekend and your mother and I would like for you to join us."

Kylee was not in the mood to be around Tony unless she was getting paid to be. And she really wasn't in the mood to be in the midst of all his perverted old friends. They always made her feel uncomfortable by staring at her like she was a piece of meat. Plus, 2 Chainz was supposed to be performing at Skate-A-Mania later the same night.

"Daddy, I really don't feel like bein' bothered with Uncle Tony and all his friends. So I think I'll pass," Kylee said.

"What's wrong with Tony's friends? They're genuine, down-to-earth, well-rounded men," her father stated.

"They're well-rounded all right." Kylee laughed, referring to the majority of his friends' shapes.

"Kylee, you ain't right," her father reprimanded her.

"I'm jus' sayin'." She chuckled.

"Anyways, we want you to be there."

"Who all gon' be there?" Kylee huffed, not really wanting to go. She knew in a couple of months she would be off to college, so spending a little quality time with her parents and their weird friends wouldn't be all that bad—she hoped.

"Just a few friends of Tony's and mines from the office, Sylvia and a couple of her friends, I'm assuming," her father said, before mentioning a few other who were planning on attending.

"Sylvia comin' huh?" Kylee asked, before twisting up her face.

"Why wouldn't she? It is her house too," Kylee's father stated.

"I know, Daddy, I was just askin'," Kylee said, trying to disguise the hatred she held for Tony's fake-ass wife, Sylvia.

"Oh, and I'reon gon' be there too," her father added.

"Oh wow, I haven't seen her in forever. Is she still goin' to that all-girls boarding school in Spain?" Kylee asked.

"She actually graduated about two weeks ago, so she's coming home Friday for good," her father said.

"That's what's up!" Kylee said, smiling, quickly reminiscing about all the mischief she, Ja'Nay, and I'reon used to get into.

"I never understood why Tony and Sylvia sent that girl away to Spain just to go to school," her father rambled. "I understand she was getting way out of hand, but there are plenty of boarding schools here in the United States they could have sent her to." Kylee's father shook his head in disgust.

Kylee knew exactly where this conversation was heading. She was tired of justifying the reason behind her wanting to go way across the country just to go to college. "Okay, Dad, I gotta go. I'll see you and Mom Saturday. I love you," she said before quickly hanging up. Kylee smiled and shook her head before continuing her workout.

Chapter Four

It was late Saturday afternoon by the time Kylee finally dragged herself out of bed. She needed the extra rest from the busy week she'd had. Spending the last four days with Cedric, Vaughn, Joshua, and Antoine had her feeling completely drained, but the money and gifts she received on top of the fun she had with each one were well worth it.

After making herself a quick brunch, Kylee thought about going back to bed, but knew her parents wouldn't have it, so to keep from hearing their mouths she took a quick shower before finding herself something to wear. Kylee was rushing around the house, making sure she had everything she needed, when Tupac's "Dear Mama" starting playing on her cell phone.

Kylee walked over and picked her phone up off her nightstand. "Hey, Mom, what's up?" she answered as she still fumbled around her bedroom.

"Where are you?" her mother started in.

"I'm comin' Mom, dang," Kylee huffed as she looked around her room.

"When, Kylee? You were supposed to be here over an hour ago," her mother fussed.

"I'll be there in about twenty minutes, Mommy," Kylee replied before pushing the end button on her cell phone and tossing it in her purse. She was running late as usual, but this time it was on purpose. Listening to the same stories her father and his friends shared at every event since she was little, about how many women they'd slept with in their heyday, was not something Kylee was interested in hearing. She continued walking around the house, making sure she had everything, before stopping in front of the full-length mirror that hung on the hallway wall.

"My goodness, girl, if you get any finer . . ." she said to her reflection as she checked herself out from every angle. She walked back into her bedroom and grabbed from the closet her all-white skates with the pink strings and pink fluffy balls and threw them over her shoulder. She would need these later on for the party at the skating rink. Kylee planned on being front and center for the 2 Chainz performance. She then grabbed her Louis Vuitton overnight bag with her skating clothes in it and headed out to the car.

"Hey, Kylee," Mr. Vernon, her eighty-year-old neighbor, hollered out as she locked her front door.

"Hey, Mr. Vernon." Kylee looked over and waved.

"You sho'll lookin' good today." He smirked as his old dessert bone attempted to pulsate a few times.

Kylee sported a pair of tight dark denim Rock Star jeans with the worn look, with a white, sheer Burberry shirt with a royal blue camisole underneath. Her ears dripped with the four-carat diamond earrings that Tony had gotten her for one of her graduation gifts and her wrist sparkled with the matching tennis bracelet. Last but not least, she wore a pair of six-inch royal blue Burak Uyan open-toe sandals to top off her attire.

Kylee smiled. "Thank you, Mr. Vernon," she replied.

"You got a date or somethin'?" he pried as he recklessly eyeballed her.

"No, my godfather is havin' a cookout," she answered as she made her way down the walk.

"You goin' to a cookout dressed like that?" he asked.

Damn, this old-ass nigga is nosey as hell, Kylee thought before answering. "Yes, Mr. Vernon."

Kylee hit the button on her key ring, unlocking her car doors.

"Well why you need them skates if you goin' to a cookout?" Mr. Vernon pried.

Damn, what the fuck? Kylee thought, ignoring Mr. Vernon's question and continuing to her car.

"Now you know if I was twenty years younger I would give you a run for your money," Mr. Vernon said as Kylee opened her car door.

Kylee stopped in her tracks and smiled over at Mr. Vernon. "If I didn't know any better Mr. Vernon, I would think you were flirtin' wit' me."

"I am. Is it workin'?" he asked hopefully.

Kylee looked over at Mr. Vernon, who looked like he had one foot in the grave and the other on a banana peel, and shook her head no. She tossed her overnight bag and skates in the back seat before turning her attention back to her neighbor. "Mr. Vernon, you old enough to be my granddaddy," Kylee said, letting him down respectfully as she knew how.

"I understand all that, but if you give me five minutes of your time, I can have you callin' me granddaddy." Mr. Vernon smirked wickedly.

Kylee's eyes widened. "Mr. Vernon." She laughed. "I didn't know you talked like that!"

"I'm what you call an ol' school freak," Mr. Vernon said, grabbing his manhood.

"Oh my goodness, Mr. Vernon!" Kylee laughed as she got in her car and shut the door. She shook her head before starting the car. "Damn, I'm on E." Kylee still had a smiled plastered on her face as she pulled out the driveway, still not believing Mr. Vernon's actions. Usher's "Climax" was on the radio. Kylee turned up the music as loud as it would go before heading to the gas station on a hope and a prayer.

Kylee pulled up in the crowded gas station and had to wait because there wasn't an available pump. "Damn, everybody must be on E," she said, waiting for someone to pull off. Her cell phone began to ring as she waited impatiently. She dug in her purse, pulled it out, and checked the caller ID.

"What's up?" she answered with a smile.

"Am I gon' see you tonight after the skating party?" Ricco asked.

"Yep, you sure are," Kylee answered as she pulled up in front of an available pump and shut the engine off.

"Cool. My wife don't have to work tonight so I'ma get us a room at the Motel 6," Ricco said.

"Motel 6?" Kylee asked with a frown. "Do I look like a Motel 6 typa bitch to you?" she asked boldly.

"Naw, baby, but I had to pay my car note and pay somethin' on my son's braces, so I don't really have much money left outta my check," Ricco explained.

"Oh, well I don't know what to tell you then, 'cause Kylee Ny'Air Hampton don't do cheap motels," she stated bluntly. "And another thing, you thought you was bouta fuck me for free? You didn't even plan on feedin' me first?"

"Damn, baby, how come I just can't get one on the house?" Ricco asked desperately. "Or just let me make it up to you next week when I get paid."

"You know I don't fuck for free! Plus, I just got my hair done and you think I'm about to let you sweat it out for nothin'?"

"I said I'll make it up to you when I get my check next week, I swear," he pleaded.

"Then just holla at me next week when you get paid," Kylee stated.

"I woulda had the money today but I told you what I had to pay," Ricco said, hoping Kylee would understand.

"So, what the fuck your car note and your son's braces have to do wit' me?" she snapped uncaringly.

Kylee knew when she first met Ricco that he wasn't ballin' like all the rest of the niggas she was used to messing around with, but his charm and good looks had her intrigued, but game and looks alone just weren't gon' cut it. It wasn't like she didn't let him know what she was about from the gate so there was no excuse!

"So you really gon' play me like that?" Ricco asked quietly.

"No, you're playin' yourself like that," she shot before pushing the end button on her phone and tossing it back in her purse. Kylee threw her purse strap over her shoulder, opened the car door, and got out feeling a little disappointed because she'd been looking forward to feeling all eight and three-quarters of Ricco's pipe up inside of her. Kylee wasn't about to start breaking her rules and fucking for free; if she did it once, she was quite sure Ricco would expect her to continue to do it, and that wasn't happening.

Kylee caught the attention of every man and the majority of the women as she sashayed her way into the gas station, some good some bad, but she didn't care. Kylee was undeniably fine and she had no problem with letting people know that she was fully aware of it. Standing five foot six with the body of a model, her short, naturally curly hair was always intact. Her almond-shaped eyes matched her cinnamon complexion, which always had a glow to it, and was flawless, along with a set of the deepest dimples. Her entire look had some swearing she was mixed with something. She walked over to the pop cooler, opened it up, and grabbed a Faygo red pop.

"Hey, baby, can I holla at you for a minute?" asked some cat grabbing a twenty-four-ounce can of Maverick from the cooler beside Kylee.

Kylee could tell by the drink in his hand that this nigga was broke. "I'm cool." She grimaced, letting the cooler door slam shut and making her way up the aisle and over to the Slim Jims.

"What's your name?" another guy asked, with a pack of diapers in one hand and a box of condoms in the other.

It's a li'l too late for them, Kylee thought, referring to the condoms, ignoring his question.

"Stuck-up bitch," the guy spat.

Any other time Kylee would have responded with a verbal tongue-lashing, but she wasn't about to waste her time arguing with a nothing-ass nigga; she had important places to be.

Kylee grabbed a couple of Slim Jims and walked up to the front of the gas station and stood in the long line. She waited impatiently as the cashier took his sweet time ringing up each customer.

OMG, what's takin' this asshole so long? she thought as she shifted her weight from one foot to the other. Kylee kept glancing out the door at her car to make sure no one was bothering it. She couldn't chance leaving her baby unattended for too long. *Not around all these thug-ass niggas who be hanging out at this gas station.*

"Finally," she mumbled when another cashier came out from the back to help out. Kylee could hear two men behind her discussing how good her ass looked in her jeans. She tried her hardest to ignore them until she heard one of the men say he bet she had some good pussy. Just as she was about to turn around and serve them like a Sunday dinner, the bell chimed over the door, making her turn her attention toward the sound.

Kylee instantly forgot about the two bums behind her as this fine piece of meat walked through the door. She was never one to believe in love at first sight, but this fine specimen of a man had her believing otherwise. Kylee had never seen a man this handsome before; actually she didn't think it was possible for anyone to be this fine. The love of her life stood at least six foot one, with a muscular build that had to have come from a regular workout; his caramel skin was as smooth as Barry White's voice. He had long, shiny, thick, well-maintained locks that hung neatly to the middle of his back. His line-up and goatee were both on point. Kylee could see the cuts in his arms and chest through the tight-fitting Ed Hardy shirt he was wearing. Tattoos covered his arms like sleeves on a shirt. Kylee could tell by his getup that dude wasn't no slouch. He was a walking gift, one Kylee wanted the chance to unwrap. This dude had Kylee so mesmerized she didn't even hear the cashier ask if he could help her.

"Can I help you? Dang," the cashier shot, snapping Kylee out of her trance.

"I think I forgot something," Kylee said, placing her pop and Slim Jims on the counter and getting out of line, so she could get the attention of this sexy mystery man.

The guy was standing in the cooler, trying to decide what type of water to buy, as Kylee strutted over toward him. Kylee was intrigued by this man's sex appeal, and was about to start up a conversation with him until he opened his mouth, beating her to the punch.

"What kind of water you want, baby?" he asked in a thick Jamaican accent.

For a quick second Kylee thought he was talking to her until she looked over her shoulder and saw a female walking their way.

"I don't care," she replied with a smile, walking over and standing beside him.

The guy glanced over at Kylee for a quick second before turning his attention back to his chick.

No, this nigga did not just look at me like I'm average or something, Kylee thought as she walked over to the cooler next to them. She could smell the soft scent of coconut conditioner coming from his locks as she walked past him. She opened up the cooler and pretended to be looking for something to drink herself.

Kylee got slightly jealous as she watched the two interact with each other.

"I like the cranberry Vitamin Water," Kylee intervened, trying to get this guy's attention any way she could.

The couple looked at Kylee and smiled. "Thank you," they both said simultaneously before deciding to taking Kylee's advice and grabbing the cranberry Vitamin Waters before walking away.

Kylee was not used to men not paying her any attention. Even if they were with their women, they would always find a discreet way to at least try to check out her backyard, but this guy didn't even give her a second look, making Kylee second-guess her pimpin' game. *This might be a challenge,* Kylee thought. Kylee loved a challenge though, and she wasn't leaving until she got some type of reaction from this man.

Kylee peeked over the shelves to see what aisle this guy and his chick were in. Once she saw that they were three aisles over by the chips, she made her way over to where they were. As Kylee turned down their aisle, she was relieved when the girl answered her ringing cell phone. By the tone of her conversation it was one of her girlfriends, and if her friendship was anything like her and Ja'Nay's this chick wouldn't be paying any attention to her man.

Good, Kylee thought. Kylee grabbed a bag of Funyuns as she headed up the aisle. Denzel— what she would call him for right now—shot her a crooked smile that instantly made her panties wet. She smiled back and continued walking past, smelling the same coconut scent. She purposely dropped her bag of chips on the floor. If this guy was a real man, he was watching, so she slowly bent down and picked them up. She looked back at him, and smiled again before continuing her way up to the register.

"That's what I'm talkin' about," she said with a cocky attitude as she stood in line, smiling at her accomplished mission.

Chapter Five

Kylee was bumping her theme song, "Ego" by Beyoncé, on repeat as she thought about this mystery man the entire ride to her godfather's house. She never thought with her looks that trying to get a man's attention would be like pulling teeth. To keep her self-esteem on ten, Kylee brushed it off as him showing his girl respect. She knew deep down that if she ever ran into him by himself she could work her magic with no interruptions and that would be all she wrote. She would surely have all of his attention. Kylee was so far in thought she drove right past Tony's house.

"Oh, shit!" Kylee laughed once she realized what she had done. "Damn, this nigga got me zonin'," she said, busting a U-turn in the driveway three doors down from Tony.

Kylee pulled up in the crowded horseshoe driveway and parked behind her father's Aston Martin. She pulled down the visor and checked her makeup before getting out. It seemed like it took forever to make it to the front door. Once she did, she rang the doorbell and waited as the long, drawn-out song chimed. She could hear the music from the live jazz band playing in the backyard.

"Good evening, Señorita Kylee," Marta said, answering the door.

"Hey, Marta," Kylee replied.

"Everybody's out back." Marta led Kylee out where the rest of the guests were gathered. "Señorita Kylee is here," Marta announced once they made it to the patio. No one paid Marta's announcement any attention and continued partying.

Why is this broad announcing my entrance? I know I'm a star and all, Kylee thought. Kylee walked out on the patio. There were people everywhere, laughing, talking, and having themselves a good old time. Kylee was impressed but not surprised by how Tony had transformed his backyard. He had several buffet tables of food of all kinds; there were waiters walking around in those little white jackets, serving expensive bottles of champagne; and a dance floor was built on top of his swimming pool with different-colored pastel lights that were flashing to the beat of the music. If Tony didn't know how to do anything else, he sure knew how to throw a party. Kylee was searching the crowd for her parents when she heard someone scream her name.

"Kylee," her god-sister squealed and ran toward her with open arms.

"I'reon?" Kylee smiled widely and met her halfway.

"Oh my goodness, it's been forever," I'reon said, wrapping her arms around her and hugging her tight.

"I know, wow," Kylee said while hugging her back.

"I'm feelin' the short do. It looks good on you," I'reon stepped back and complimented her.

"Thanks. But you know I can rock any style and make it look good," Kylee said, running her hand down her wavy hair.

"I see you still conceited as hell." I'reon laughed.

"And you know this." Kylee laughed too.

"Look at you. You still look good, straight model material. The men and the women would love you over in Spain." I'reon smiled.

"You think so?" Kylee said before striking a pose.

"You silly, girl." I'reon laughed.

"You look good too, girl. You know they've always said we looked alike," Kylee said.

"Right, but we never thought so. I always thought I looked better than you," I'reon joked. I'reon and Kylee were the spitting image of each other right down to their deep dimples; only differences were I'reon was a shade lighter than Kylee and about an inch shorter, and thicker in the waist with long, wavy hair that she kept neatly in a ponytail.

"You wish." Kylee laughed.

"Where's Ja'Nay?" I'reon asked. "How come she didn't come?"

"She at home. She wanted to come too, but Me'andra wasn't finished doing her sew-in. She told me to tell you hi and can't wait to kick it wit' you," Kylee said.

"Man, I would have loved to see her," I'reon said, disappointed.

"Speakin' of kickin' it, they havin' a skating party tonight at Skate-A-Mania. You rollin' wit' us or what?" Kylee asked.

"Man, sure sounds like fun." I'reon contemplated it. "But I can't."

"Why not? Don't tell me you done went over to Spain and got too bourgeois to kick it wit' ya girls!"

"Now you know better than that. It's just I have company and I know they wouldn't feel comfortable goin' and I can't leave 'em here wit' my parents as bad as I want to," I'reon replied.

"Who is it? Ya dude?"

"Somethin' like that." I'reon smiled. "Speakin' of dudes, have you settled down yet or are you still playin' niggas like a game of tonk?"

"I'm still doin' what I do best," Kylee admitted. "You know I'm not the settlin' type. What about you?"

"Yeah, I finally found somebody to sit me down for the time bein'," I'reon said happily.

"Well, where he at? I need to meet this nigga," Kylee said.

"Shawn, *ven aqui*," I'reon said, waving.

Kylee was confused as she watched as a big, burly, manly looking female wearing a baseball cap and baggy jean shorts walked toward them.

"Please tell me this is not your girlfriend," Kylee whispered.

"Nope, she's not," I'reon replied.

"Thank God," Kylee said, relieved.

"She's my boyfriend," I'reon replied with a smile.

"What?" Kylee asked, shocked, and wanted to say more but Shawn was now standing in front of them.

"Shawn, *este es mi de Dios hermana, Kylee*," I'reon introduced.

"What did you just say? All I understood was my name," Kylee asked with a confused look on her face.

"I told Shawn that you were my god-sister," I'reon translated. "Shawn doesn't speak any English."

Shawn stuck out her hand for Kylee to shake. "*Mucho gusto.*"

Damn, look at this broad's hand. I'reon always did know how to pick 'em, Kylee thought. "What she say?" Kylee looked over at I'reon and asked.

"She said nice to meet you," I'reon responded.

"Oh, okay. And la cucaracha to you too," Kylee replied sarcastically before placing her tiny hand inside of Shawn's.

Shawn had a puzzled look on her face as Kylee and I'reon laughed at Kylee's quip.

"*Ignorar ella, ella es un poco loco,*" I'reon said to Shawn.

"What you say about me, heffa?" Kylee asked I'reon.

"I told Shawn to ignore you, 'cause you a little crazy." I'reon laughed.

"Oh, okay. I thought you were callin' me a bitch or somethin'," Kylee joked with a smile.

"*Usted tiene una sonrisa bonita. Ustedes dos se parecen,*" Shawn replied with a huge smile.

"What *she* or *he* say?" Kylee asked, slightly annoyed because she couldn't understand what Shawn was saying.

"*She* said you have a nice smile and we look alike," I'reon repeated.

"Is yo' dude tryin'a hit on me?" Kylee questioned.

"Naw, fool. She just thinks you have a pretty smile. What's wrong wit' that?" I'reon asked.

"You really want me to answer that?"

I'reon shook her head and laughed. "No, please don't."

"I'm goin' over here to speak to my parents. I'll talk to you later." Kylee laughed too, before grabbing a glass of champagne off the tray as one of the waiters walked past before heading off to find her parents. Kylee really wasn't feeling I'reon's idea of her messing around with another female, but she really wasn't surprised by her decision. I'reon always had to be the first to try something new and enjoyed experimenting with all different type of things such as drugs, alcohol, and exotic foods, and this situation was no different.

Kylee spotted her parents sitting at a table, engaged in a conversation with Tony, Sylvia, and some other guest. She quickly drank down her champagne and set the glass on an empty table before heading over.

"Hey, there goes my baby." Kylee's mom stood from her seat and smiled happily when she spotted her daughter.

"Hey, Mommy." Kylee smiled back, giving her mother a tight hug.

"About time you got here," her father said.

Kylee rolled her eyes. She knew her dad had been drinking so to avoid an argument Kylee spoke and left it at that. "Hey, Dad."

"Don't pay him any attention, he's drunk." Kylee's mom laughed, before sitting back down.

"I'm grown aren't I?" her father asked smartly.

Kylee looked over at her father with a mug on her face. She hoped her father wasn't about to start trippin' on her mother like he usually did after a few drinks. Here lately her father had been drinking and disrespecting her mother more than usual. Kylee had it set in her mind that if her father got to talking crazy to her mother in front of all these people, that she was gon' flip straight gangsta on him. It was bad enough he disrespected her in the privacy of their home, but lately he'd been feeling real jazzy and been trying to disrespect her in front of people. Kylee knew when she was younger there wasn't much she could say, but she was grown now; what was he going to do, send her to her room?

"Hey, come give your Uncle Tony a hug and a kiss," Tony slurred, noticing the ill look on Kylee's face.

Kylee walked over to Tony, and gave him a hug and a quick peck on the cheek.

"Hey, Sylvia," Kylee threw her hand up and said. She didn't want to, but out of respect for it being her house too, she did.

"Hey, Kylee," Sylvia spoke back.

Kylee walked over and sat down next to her mother.

"I love your hair like this. I'm glad you took that front lace outta your head," her mother said, running her hand down her daughter's wavy mane.

"It's called a lace-front, Mommy." Kylee laughed.

"Whatever. You should keep your hair like this," her mother suggested.

"I told her she was model material." I'reon intervened in their conversation as she walked over and sat next to Kylee.

"Girl, I don't have time to be modelin'. I'm gettin' ready to go to college in the fall," Kylee stated.

"That's right," her father said, butting in.

Kylee smacked her lips. "Anyways."

"Shoot, I don't see why not. You got the looks, the height, and you hip to the latest fashion. You got good taste. You got to have 'cause I see you rockin' them Burak Uyans and them thousand-dollar shoes. Don't too many people know about those over here in the States," I'reon said.

Kylee's dad nearly choked on his drink before speaking. "A thousand dollars? Where you get that kinda money at for some shoes?" her father asked, skeptical.

"Yeah, I'm wit' your father on that." Her mother frowned.

"These are knockoffs," Kylee replied nervously.

"No, sis, fashion is what I studied over in Spain and I know knockoffs when I see 'em, and them there," I'reon said, pointing down to Kylee's shoes, "ain't no knockoffs."

"Yeah, they are," Kylee said between clenched teeth.

"Okay, if you say so," I'reon said, standing up. "I'm goin' to fix me a plate; anybody else want anything?"

"Get up and go fix me a plate," Kylee's father looked over at his wife and demanded.

Kylee waited to see what her mother was going to do before she intervened in grown folks' conversation. Kylee's mother didn't hesitate to stand up.

"I'm goin' over to fix me a plate, Uncle Vince. I can just grab you somethin' while I'm over there," I'reon said

"Naw, I want Vivian to fix my plate." He scowled.

"Ain't that what Marta gets paid for?" Kylee frowned.

"I'll get it," her mother said quickly.

"You ain't his maid," Kylee huffed.

"You betta stay in a child's place," her father warned.

I'reon, Tony, and Sylvia all had confused looks on their faces.

"I'm grown," Kylee mumbled before walking away.

"She done got too grown for her britches," her father fussed, before picking up his glass of Hennessy and tossing it back.

Kylee walked over and took a seat at the bar. She needed to get as far away from her father as possible before she ended up saying something she would later regret. She ordered herself a shot of St. Claire Green Tea Vodka mixed with Simply Lemonade with Raspberry. She bobbed her head to the music as she sipped on her drink.

"You okay over here?" Sylvia walked up, placed her hand on Kylee's shoulder, and asked.

Kylee quickly moved her shoulder, making Sylvia's hand fall. "I'm good," Kylee said with an attitude, not wanting to be bothered with her or anyone else.

"Nice earrings. I have a pair just like them," Sylvia antagonized her.

"What do you want, Sylvia?" Kylee looked at her and asked.

"Look, Kylee, I already know you don't like me, but I don't know why. I have never done anything to you. Besides, you're the one who's fuckin' my husband, so I should be the one who has the problem with you," Sylvia said.

Kylee sat calmly and continued sipping on her drink. "And you sayin' that to say what?"

"I'm not really sayin' it to say anything. I just want you to know that I'm fully aware of what's goin' on between you and my husband, that's all," Sylvia said.

"So what you gon' do, tell my dad on me?" Kylee inquired.

"Your father would be crushed if he found out that his sweet, innocent little girl was fuckin' one of his best friends." Sylvia grimaced. "That's the only reason why I haven't told him . . . yet."

"Do you really think I give a fuck about you tellin' my dad? What the fuck he gon' do to me? I'm grown," Kylee spat.

"Well you weren't when y'all started messin' around," Sylvia stated.

"Don't threaten me," Kylee warned.

"Oh, I'm not threatenin' you. I'm just lettin' you know that eventually I'm gon' have to tell your father what's goin' on between you and Tony."

"Look, why are you over here botherin' me with this nonsense?" Kylee asked smartly.

"I just came to check on you, that's all." Sylvia smirked before turning to walk away.

"Hey, Sylvia," Kylee called over her shoulder. Sylvia stopped and turned around. "When you do decide to tell my dad about me and Tony, make sure you tell Tony about you and my dad!"

"What did you just say?" Sylvia asked, surprised, making sure she'd heard right and wondering how Kylee had found out about her and Vince's affair.

"You heard me," Kylee said before finishing off her drink. Kylee swung around on the barstool to face Sylvia. "Now how do you think Tony would feel if he found out about that? I don't think he would like that too well; do you?"

"I don't know what you're talkin' about," Sylvia stated nervously.

"You might not know, but I do. But don't worry, your secret is safe wit' me." Kylee winked.

Sylvia had to play it cool. She didn't want to say anything else to piss Kylee off more than she already had, because she knew better than anybody that if Tony found out she was cheating on him he would surely kill her and Vince, and wouldn't think twice about it.

"Suit yourself. Keep fuckin' Tony all you want. You're the one who's gon' regret it in the end," Sylvia said before turning to walk away.

"I planned on it. I didn't need your permission," Kylee said victoriously, not knowing or caring what Sylvia meant by her last remark.

"What you two over here talkin' about?" I'reon walked up and asked, quickly sensing the awkwardness. "What did I just walk into?"

"Nothin'. I was just over here asking Kylee about her college plans, that's all," Sylvia lied.

"Oh, okay. Well you gon' have to tell me all about 'em too, but right now I gotta go rescue Shawn from Hector; he can't keep his hands off her." I'reon laughed.

"You might need some help." Sylvia laughed too, wanting to get away from Kylee.

"Yeah, you're right, come on," I'reon said, grabbing her mother by the hand and leading her over to the dance floor.

Kylee watched as I'reon and Sylvia walked away. She then took a look around at the other guests and shook her head. She couldn't believe how they were walking around acting as if they lived perfect lives when half of them were alcoholics, addicted to drugs, or in the closet, and the other half were cheaters, gamblers, or mentally messed up in the head. The more Kylee looked around the more she couldn't wait to go away to college. Kylee couldn't take it any longer; she'd had enough of this atmosphere. She needed to get away from here. She turned around, ordered herself another drink, and took it to the head. She then slid the bartender a twenty dollar tip before heading to her car.

Chapter Six

Kylee was sprawled out in her bed, sleeping like a newborn baby, until she was awakened by the rumbling noise of a lawn mower, that sounded like it was at the foot of her bed. Irritated, she rolled over to check the time on her cell phone.

"Damn, Mr. Vernon, it's six o'clock A.M.," Kylee shouted angrily. She picked up her pillow and covered her head, trying her hardest to drown out the noise, but it was no use.

Kylee's head was pounding from the one too many drinks she and Ja'Nay had drunk at the after hour the night before and the loud noise wasn't making it any better.

Kylee lay motionless until she couldn't take it anymore. She threw her cover back and got out of bed. "I'm about to cuss this old mutha-fucka out!" Kylee put on her robe and slippers, walked out of her bedroom, and headed down the stairs. "He is so fuckin' rude! He coulda waited 'til at least eleven o'clock to cut his damn grass like he always does," Kylee fussed while wiping the sleep out of her eyes. She walked out the front door, not caring what she looked like for the first time, and went next door. She spotted a lawn-care truck in Mr. Vernon's driveway.

"Kingston's Landscaping Service, huh?" Kylee said, reading the sign on the side of the truck. "He must have hired someone to cut his grass. I'll tell you what if he don't wait until later on to cut this grass I'm gon' call this muthafucka's boss and have his job!" Kylee walked up in Mr. Vernon's yard with a serious attitude. She could tell from behind that the man riding on the zero-turn lawn mower surely wasn't Mr. Vernon, but she couldn't have cared less if it was Barack Obama; she was about to let this nigga have it.

"Excuse me," Kylee snapped snottily. The gentleman continued cutting grass while bobbing his head. "Excuse me," Kylee shouted again but this time a little louder, after noticing the guy was wearing headphones.

The gentleman finally turned around, shut the engine off, slid his Dre Beats headphones to the back of his neck, and smiled. "May I help you?" he asked in his native tongue.

Oh my fuckin' goodness! This is the nigga from the gas station, Kylee thought, instantly becoming embarrassed by her appearance.

"Umm, ummm, yeah," Kylee stammered as her demeanor softened. Her train of thought had clearly derailed. It took a few seconds for her mind to get back on track. "Good mornin'."

"Good mornin'," he replied with a smile. "What can I do for you, ma?"

"Ummm, my name is Kylee and I live next door and I'm up there tryin'a sleep," she rambled, while pointing to her bedroom window. "I was just wonderin' if you could wait a little while longer before you cut the grass. The noise from the lawnmower is kinda keepin' me up."

The guy looked at Kylee from the top of her head scarf to the bottom of her Angry Bird slippers. "You said Kylee eh?" he asked, making sure he got her name correct.

"Yes," she replied nervously.

Under any other circumstances he would have told a person requesting how and when to do his job to go to hell, but how could he say no to the pretty face standing before him? "I think I can do that for you." He smiled.

His smile made Kylee's heart flutter. "Thank you so much." She smiled back gratefully before quickly turning to walk away, still embarrassed by the way she looked; she had definitely got caught slippin'.

"No problem," he said, watching as she headed back over to her own yard. He shook his head and smiled before heading to his truck to grab hedge trimmers.

Kylee walked back into her condo giddy as ever. She wanted badly to stay and flirt with the sexy lawn guy, especially since his girl wasn't around, but her pounding head wouldn't allow her to. She walked into the kitchen, grabbed a bottle of Tylenol out of the cabinet, and opened it before pouring herself a glass of orange juice. Kylee popped two pills in her mouth, drank her juice straight down and headed back to her bedroom. She climbed into bed and closed her eyes.

She tried hard to go back to sleep, but couldn't. Her thoughts stayed on the lawn guy with the sexy Jamaican accent. After about twenty minutes of tossing and turning, Kylee opened her eyes and climbed out of bed. She walked over to her bedroom window and discreetly looked down at the lawn guy while he trimmed Mr. Vernon's hedges. She watched as he wiped the pouring sweat from his forehead.

Damn, he looks so good, Kylee thought as she continued watching him work. Her mind began running wild. She began fantasizing about all the things she would have loved to do to him if she ever got the chance while watching his every move.

Kylee was so caught up; she must have blown her cover because the lawn guy looked up at her window and waved. Kylee took a quick step back. He laughed and continued working.

"Damn, I hope this nigga don't think I'm a stalker." Kylee giggled. "Oh well, I guess since I can't go back to sleep I might as well get my workout in before I meet up with Ja'Nay and I'reon."

Kylee walked over and made up her bed before heading to the adjacent bathroom to shower. After showering, Kylee put on a pair of white spandex Nike running shorts, the ones that showed off every curve and then some, with the sports bra to match. She grabbed a pair of crisp white and pink Nike Lunar Eclipse running shoes out of the closet. "Forgot my socks," she said, heading over to her dresser, grabbing a pair of no-shows out of her sock drawer before quickly peeking out her window, to see if Denzel was still over there working. After getting dressed, Kylee strapped her iPod on to her forearm, put her sweat towel in the front of her shorts, and headed downstairs. She walked into the kitchen, grabbing a bottle of cold water out of the refrigerator before heading out the door. She walked off her porch and headed over into Mr. Vernon's yard.

The lawn guy smiled as he watched Kylee walk over to him. "Don't tell me that my trimmers are too loud, too?" he joked as he checked out Kylee's washboard abs, perfectly shaped hips, and the colorful tattoo that decorated the entire right side of her upper body.

Kylee laughed. "No, I brought you a peace offerin'."

"What is it?" he asked, smiling.

"Here you go," she said nervously, while handing him the bottle of cold water.

"Thank you," he said, taking the water from her hand.

Kylee watched as he opened the water and took it to the head. She instantly got hot. She didn't know if it was from the smoldering sun or the way his lips gripped the rim of the water bottle; whatever it was she could definitely feel the heat.

"Good Lawd! Elizabeth, I think I'm comin' to join you honey," Mr. Vernon walked outside and said while grabbing his chest like Fred Sanford used to do.

Kylee shook her head. "Good mornin', Mr. Vernon," she spoke.

"It wasn't a good mornin' at first 'cause my bunions were on fire, my rheumatoid arthritis was actin' up in my hands, and I just found out I got gout. But seein' you in that there outfit, I think I'm healed!" Mr. Vernon smiled wickedly.

The lawn guy shook his head and smiled.

"Well, I guess I better let you get back to work," Kylee said, taking a step back, letting Mr. Vernon spoil her mood.

"Thanks again for the water, ma," he replied with a wink.

Kylee put her ear buds in, pushed play on her iPod, and took off jogging. Mr. Vernon and the lawn guy both watched Kylee until she was all the way out of their sight.

Mr. Vernon shook his head in disbelief. "Welcome to the neighborhood."

"So let me get this straight. The nigga caught you watchin' him out your bedroom window?" Ja'Nay laughed before sticking a spoonful of ICEE into her mouth as they walked around downtown to waste time before the movie started.

"Yes," Kylee answered in disbelief.

"Now you know you lose playa points for that." I'reon laughed too.

"I know." Kylee shook her head and laughed.

"Shit, the nigga probably thinks she's a stalker."
Ja'Nay giggled.

"Right," I'reon agreed.

"I know, man. I still can't believe I got caught."

"Shit, if he's as fine as you say he is, he needs to
be stalked," Ja'Nay said.

"So what's this Greek god's name?" I'reon
asked.

"She don't know," Ja'Nay answered.

"I call him Denzel," Kylee said.

"So yo' ass took him a bottle of water and you
still didn't get his name?" I'reon questioned.

"I know, I was kinda nervous," Kylee admitted.

"Nervous? Not Kylee Ny'Air Hampton," I'reon
asked, shocked.

"I'm wit' you on that," Ja'Nay said, shocked as
well.

"I know, man. It's crazy 'cause I have never
met a nigga who made me nervous. You know
usually I'm the aggressive one, but not with
Denzel."

"I still can't believe you didn't get the nigga's
name, Kylee," I'reon said.

"All I know is that he works for Kingston's
Landscaping," Kylee said, remembering the
name on the side of the truck.

"Well there it is, all you gotta do is look Kingston's
Landscaping number up in the phonebook and call
it," I'reon suggested.

"And ask for who?" Kylee asked smartly.

"Well, you can always ask for the tall, sexy nigga with locks and the Jamaican accent," Ja'Nay joked.

Ja'Nay and I'reon both laughed.

"Y'all bitches ain't no help," Kylee said, pretending to be mad.

"Awwww, my sister is in love with her neighbor's lawn guy," I'reon teased.

"I am not in love wit' him," Kylee corrected.

"Shit, I can't believe she even got a crush on him. He works for a lawn care service so you know he can't be makin' that much money," Ja'Nay said.

"Right, you know Kylee likes her niggas ballin', not just sittin' back, watchin' the game," I'reon agreed.

"That's not true. I mess wit' a guy who don't have a whole lotta money," Kylee contested.

"Yeah, but you only mess wit' him on payday." Ja'Nay laughed.

"True," Kylee agreed. "Plus it ain't like I wanna get wit' him. I just think he's fine as hell, that's all. And you guys are right; he can't be makin' that much money to be fuckin' wit' me, and if he does, he probably got a gang of kids wit' a buncha different baby mamas he has to pay child support to." Kylee started feeling turned off by the thought.

"You a straight gold-digger." I'reon laughed.

"Tell me somethin' about myself that I don't know," Kylee responded sarcastically. "I'm pretty sure Shawn's bank account ain't runnin' on E."

"You damn right it ain't," I'reon said, rolling her eyes.

"Speakin' of Shawn, when did you decide to start munchin' on carpet?" Ja'Nay inquired, finishing off her ICEE and tossing the empty cup into the trash can.

"Ewww, why you make it sound so nasty?" I'reon asked.

"It kinda is," Ja'Nay responded.

"Havin' sex wit' a woman was one of the things on my bucket list, if you really must know," I'reon admitted. "I tried it and I liked it. So now I'm wit' Shawn, but don't get it fucked up. I still love me some dick!"

"Damn, bitch, how come you can't have some ordinary shit on ya bucket list like skydivin', swimmin' wit' dolphins, or some shit like that." Ja'Nay laughed.

"You got yo' bucket list and I got mines," I'reon said, playfully rolling her eyes.

"She's right," Kylee stated.

"Well would you ever fuck wit' a bitch?" Ja'Nay asked Kylee.

Kylee thought for a brief moment. "It all depends."

"On what?" Ja'Nay and I'reon asked simultaneously. They were both surprised by Kylee's response.

"On how much she willin' to pay," Kylee answered. "But, we couldn't be seen in public. And it would have to stay behind closed doors."

"Damn, both of my friends are fucked up," Ja'Nay said, shaking her head.

"Whatever." Kylee laughed.

"Don't knock it until you try it," I'reon said.

"I'll pass. I'll just take yo' word for it," Ja'Nay said, turning up her nose.

"Look, they have a new shop over there," Kylee said, pointing.

"Yeah, that's the one I was tellin' you about the other day. You don't pay me no damn attention," Ja'Nay huffed.

"I remember you talkin' about a store, but you're right, I wasn't payin' you any attention." Kylee laughed.

Ja'Nay smacked her lips. "Anyways, I heard they sell bongs, necklaces, incense, and some other Jamaican paraphernalia up in there," Ja'Nay said.

"Ooooh, y'all wanna go check it out?" I'reon asked, excited.

"Yeah, let's go in there. We might find some shit we like," Ja'Nay said.

"Includin' a lawn guy." I'reon smirked.

"Shut up and let's go." Kylee laughed as they all walked across the street.

Kylee, Ja'Nay, and I'reon walked inside the Jamaican shop. Julian Marley's "Boom Draw" was playing.

"This is my cut," I'reon said, bobbing her head to the music as she browsed.

"Look at this," Kylee said, picking up a dick-shaped bong, showing her friends.

"Let's buy it." Ja'Nay laughed.

"Welcome to Sy'onn's . Can I help you?" a man appeared from behind a black curtain and asked, scaring Kylee nearly half to death.

"Oh, shit." Kylee grimaced, while holding her chest. "We just lookin'." Kylee, Ja'Nay, and I'reon all looked at the man as if he were an alien. They had seen some weird-looking folks in their day but none quite like this guy. He was at least six foot four, black as coal, with thick, matted locks that came past his knees, with the prettiest blue eyes they'd ever seen.

"Okay, let me know if I can help," he said before walking away to help some of the other customers who had just walked inside the shop.

"He looks like an alien," Ja'Nay whispered.

"I know," I'reon whispered back.

"They have some interesting stuff in here," Ja'Nay said, sniffing the different incense and picking out the ones she liked.

"Look at me, I'm a Rastafarian," I'reon joked as she put on a hat with fake locks hanging from it.

Kylee and Ja'Nay began cracking up. "You a damn fool," Kylee said.

"Come on, let's get outta here; the movie starts in an hour," I'reon said while placing the hat back on the shelf.

"Are you ladies all right out here?" another worker came from the back and asked with a smile.

"We coo . . ." Kylee turned around and hesitated, not believing it was Mr. Vernon's lawn guy. What were the chances of running into him twice in one day? *This has got to be a sign,* Kylee thought.

"Damn this nigga fine," Ja'Nay said under her breath as she sized him up.

"I'm wit' you on that," I'reon agreed checking out the man with the Jamaican accent.

"Kylee, right?" he asked.

Kylee shook her head yes. Ja'Nay and I'reon both had confused looks on their faces, wondering where Kylee knew this dude from.

"I'm beginnin' to think you followin' me," he said with a smile.

"No, honestly, I'm not. Me and my girls was just walkin' around and wanted to come in here to see what they had," she started explaining.

"Calm down, ma, I was just jokin'." He laughed, cutting Kylee off.

"Umm ummmmm," I'reon said, pretending to clear her throat.

"Hi, I'm Ja'Nay, and you are?" she asked, holding her hand out for him to shake.

"Eli." He smiled while shaking her hand.

"Okay, Eli, that's a cute name. But, um how you know my sister?" I'reon questioned.

"And how come I don't know you? Where she been hidin' you at?" Ja'Nay added.

"Calm down, y'all." Kylee laughed. "This is my neighbor's *lawn guy*," she said with big eyes.

"Ohhhhh, so you the infamous lawn guy," I'reon said, giving him her stamp of approval.

Eli was confused.

"Can you come cut my grass?" Ja'Nay joked.

"Please, excuse my friends," Kylee said, shaking her head. "They a little crazy."

"It's okay, I can tell they like to have fun," Eli said, smiling.

"Let's go look at the necklaces. Nice to finally meet you, Eli," I'reon said before grabbing

Ja'Nay by the arm and leading her off, leaving Kylee and Eli alone.

There was an awkward silence.

"So, did you ladies find everything all right?" he finally asked.

"Yeah, this is a nice store. You work here, too?" Kylee asked, looking around.

"Yep. I work here, too."

"Dang, I guess it's true when they say Jamaicans be working three and four jobs at a time huh?" Kylee asked.

"That's not always the case." Eli laughed. "We have lazy Jamaicans, too."

"Sorry," Kylee said, realizing she was stereotyping Jamaican people.

"Don't be. You can only speak about what you hear." Eli smiled.

"Eh, Eli, I'm about to run get me somethin' to eat. You want somethin' while I'm out?" the tall alien-looking guy walked over and asked.

Eli shook his head no. "I'm good."

"Okay, I'll be back in a few." He looked Kylee up and down. "*Cho! Coo deh ass,*" he said before turning to walk away.

"What he say?" Kylee frowned.

"Nothin'," Eli said, shaking his head.

"He said somethin' and I wanna know what," she said, putting her hands on her hips and waiting.

"Naw, ma, you gon' get mad," Eli said, laughing.

"No, I won't," Kylee promised.

"Naw, I'm not gon' tell you," Eli said, shaking his head no.

"Please," Kylee begged.

"All right, ma, how about I tell you the next time I see you," Eli toyed.

"I don't believe you. And besides, who said we gon' see each other again?" Kylee asked with a cocky attitude.

"Trust me, we will."

"How you figure that?" Kylee smirked, hoping he was about to ask her out on a date.

"Did you forget that I work next door to your house?" Eli asked with smile.

"Oh yeah," Kylee replied, slightly disappointed

"Come on, sis, we need to leave if we gon' make it to the movies on time." I'reon walked over and interrupted.

"Oh, okay, here I come," Kylee said, not wanting to leave yet, at least not without exchanging phone numbers.

"What movie y'all goin' to see?" Eli asked.

"We goin' to see *Flight*. The movie with the other Denzel Washington in it." I'reon looked over at Kylee and smiled.

"I didn't know there was more than one," Eli replied.

"Oh, believe me there is," I'reon assured him.

"Okay, well don't let me hold you. Y'all enjoy the movie," Eli said.

"Thank you," Kylee said, not knowing what else to say.

Kylee stood in disbelief as Eli turned to walk away. She couldn't believe he just left without asking for her number or anything.

"So what y'all talk about?" I'reon pried once Eli was out of their sight.

"Nothin' really," Kylee said, still in shock.

"Well did you at least get his number?" Ja'Nay asked.

"Nope," Kylee replied peevishly as they all headed out of the shop.

"That's you, my man?" the alien-looking guy walked back into the shop with a bag of food and asked Eli.

Eli shook his head no. "Not yet," he said, before turning to walk away, disappearing behind the black curtain.

Chapter Seven

Kylee pulled up in her driveway, shut the engine off, and got out of the car. She looked over at Mr. Vernon's well-manicured lawn. Her heart sank as she headed up the walk because while she'd been out running errands, Eli had been next door working.

"Damn, this the second time I done missed him," she said, disappointed as she walked up the steps. It had been well over two weeks since she'd last seen Eli. Kylee opened up the screen door and watched as a business card fell to the porch. She bent down, picked it up, and read it. She then turned it over and read the note on the back of it:

Call me if you need your lawn serviced,
Eli

Kylee smiled happily as she unlocked the door. "I want more than my lawn serviced," she said and continued into the house.

Kylee threw her keys and purse on the sofa and paced back and forth through her living room while reading Eli's note over and over. She debated what would be a good time to call him; even though she didn't need her lawn serviced hearing Eli's voice would make her day. She didn't want to seem desperate and call him too soon, nor did she want to wait too long, fearing he might lose interest, but with the way she looked that was the least of her worries. After about twenty minutes of going back and forth with herself, Kylee decided to go ahead and make the call.

She pulled her cell out of her purse and dialed the number on the front of the card. Her heart raced as she waited for someone to answer.

"Kingston's Landscaping," Eli answered.

"Ummm, yes, I found this card in my door and wanted to make an appointment to get my lawn serviced," Kylee stated nervously.

"Okay, let me see what I have open." Eli smiled, recognizing Kylee's voice. He paused for a brief moment as he checked his calendar. "Okay, I have an opening for your lawn next Thursday at ten o'clock A.M. and an opening for dinner tonight at eight o'clock P.M. Will either of those times work for you?" he asked boldly.

Eli caught Kylee off-guard with his dinner invite, but that didn't stop her from accepting his offer. "Both times are fine with me," she answered happily.

"Okay, cool. I'll be by to get you at eight," Eli said.

"You want me to drive?" Kylee offered, fearing he would show up driving a hooptie or, even worse, the lawn-care truck.

"You good. I'll drive." Eli laughed.

"Are you sure?" Kylee asked again, just to be certain.

"I'm sure. Don't worry; I won't pick you up in my lawn truck." Eli laughed.

Kylee laughed too. "I know you wouldn't do that," Kylee lied, wondering how he knew what she was thinking.

"Yeah, okay," Eli joked, knowing that was her exact concern.

"I'm serious." Kylee giggled.

"I'm sure you are. Okay, ma, a customer just walked in. I'll see you at eight, okay?"

"Okay." Kylee had a huge smile on her face as she pushed the end button on her cell phone. "Ooooh, I love his accent," she moaned as she dialed Ja'Nay to tell her the good news.

"I was just about to call you," Ja'Nay answered.

"Bitch, guess what?" Kylee started.

"What?" Ja'Nay quickly asked, knowing it had to be juicy by the way Kylee started off the conversation.

"I'm goin' out to dinner wit' Eli tonight." Kylee smiled widely as she grabbed her purse and made her way upstairs to her bedroom.

"Whaaat? What happened? He caught you stalkin' him again and felt sorry for yo' butt and decided to ask you out to dinner?" Ja'Nay joked.

"Ha-ha, very funny." Kylee chuckled. "No, for your information, when I got home from Walmart, he'd left a business card in my door and told me to call him."

"Okay, now that's what I'm talkin' about! My girl is finally goin' out with the lawn guy," Ja'Nay replied happily.

"About damn time he asked me out," Kylee stated, taking a seat on her bed and lying back.

"I know right. Where he takin' you?" Ja'Nay questioned.

"Wow, I don't even know. I guess I was so happy, I didn't even think to ask," Kylee admitted, before sitting up.

"Oh my goodness. Bitch, you need to get it together." Ja'Nay laughed.

"I know." Kylee laughed too. "I don't care where he takes me. I just wanna spend some time wit' him."

"I feel you on that," Ja'Nay agreed. "Okay, well, I need to finish gettin' dressed. I'll hit you back later."

"Wait a minute," Kylee called out.

"Wassup?" Ja'Nay asked.

"I thought you said you was about to call me." Kylee stood up from her bed and walked over to her closet to find something to wear.

"I was."

"And, what did you want, Blondie?" Kylee laughed as she looked through her clothes, trying to find the perfect outfit.

"Oh yeah." Ja'Nay laughed too. "Quann called me," Ja'Nay said carefully and waited for Kylee to respond.

"What the fuck he want?" Kylee snapped.

Ja'Nay took a deep breath before speaking, because she knew this conversation was about to take a turn for the worse like any other time she mentioned Quann's name. "He called to apologize and said he wants to talk to me."

"And I know you told him to go to hell right?" Kylee asked with a serious attitude.

Ja'Nay closed her eyes. "No," she said, exasperated.

"Wow is all I can say." Kylee stopped looking through her clothes and frowned.

"Damn, Kylee. I'm sorry I can't be as cold-hearted as you. I'm not cut like that, okay? Quann made a mistake, he apologized, and I accepted it. What's the big fuckin' deal?"

"The big fuckin' deal is you caught this nigga fuckin' the same bitch he introduced to you as his sister! This bitch lived wit' him, y'all was goin' shoppin' together, out to the club, you was even babysittin' this bitch's son, and you still can't see the big fuckin' deal, huh? Damn, bitch, Stevie Wonder can see what the deal is!" Kylee snapped furiously as she paced back and forth through her bedroom.

Ja'Nay sat quietly as Kylee went ham on her like she had always done.

"I mean come on, Ja'Nay, you that pressed to have that nigga in ya life? Quann ain't shit, ain't never been shit, and ain't gon' be shit. I can't understand how come you can't see that!"

"I can, but I love him and you can't help who you fall in love wit'," Ja'Nay protested.

"But you in love by yourself, Ja'Nay. If Quann loved you like you loved him, he wouldn't be messin' around wit' all these different hoes. You deserve better," Kylee said, calming her attitude, hoping to get through to her best friend, but knowing when it came to talking to Ja'Nay about Quann, it was like talking to a brick wall.

"I deserve to be happy and if bein' wit' Quann is makin' me happy then you should be happy for me," Ja'Nay said.

"How can I be happy for you when you messin' around wit' a nigga who treats you like shit?" Kylee asked, hurt. "Do me a favor and find you a nigga who knows how to treat his woman; then I'll be happy for you."

Kylee became furious all over again. She didn't expect her best friend to be as cutthroat as she was when it came to men, but she did at least want her to grow some balls and stand up for herself and not let Quann continuously run over her.

"Well do me a favor, Kylee, you do you and let me do me, okay?" Ja'Nay stated, fed up with how her best friend always judged the decisions she made when it came to men, especially Quann. Kylee had acted the same way when Ja'Nay had dated Julio and Darnell, too. It seemed like no matter what, no one was ever good enough for Ja'Nay in Kylee's eyes.

"Okay, I got'chu. Look, I'm 'bouta get off this phone 'cause I can't stomach stupidity so I'll holla at you later," Kylee said, hanging up. The last thing Kylee wanted to do was hurt her best friend's feelings, but she didn't know what else to say or do to try to get through to her. Kylee was tired of Ja'Nay constantly letting Quann run over her and felt it was time for her best friend to take a stand. Feeling disgusted, she threw her phone on the bed, walked back over to her closet, and continued looking for something to wear.

Chapter Eight

Kylee was listening to Rihanna's "Birthday Cake" as she got ready for her date. Ja'Nay crossed her mind a time or two, but instead of calling her to apologize for always being so overbearing, she just hoped her best friend knew her intentions were all good. Kylee couldn't understand why Ja'Nay was so stuck on Quann; she could have her choice of men. Ja'Nay was gorgeous. She stood five foot five with cocoa brown skin and a shape that made even Kylee envious at times. She had big, pretty, dark brown eyes that always sparkled, and shoulder-length hair that was always intact whether she wore it natural or weaved up; Ja'Nay never left the house without looking like a five-star chick.

Kylee walked into the adjacent bathroom and turned on the shower, before getting undressed and stepping in. After showering, Kylee rubbed Olive Oil hair pudding in her hair, brushed it down to her head, and watched as it curled up, just the way she liked it. She laid the brush down and headed out of the bathroom and over to her closet. Since Kylee didn't know where Eli was taking her, she decided to put on an all-purpose outfit. She chose a chocolate brown, mustard yellow, and burnt orange block print Monsoon halter sundress, with a pair of tan and gold Chanel flip-flops. Kylee accessorized her outfit with a thin gold necklace, gold bangles, and a pair of gold shoulder-length triangular-shaped earrings.

"Get it, Kylee." She smiled at the image in the full-length standing floor mirror. She pulled her chocolate brown Michael Kors Colgate leather purse off the shelf before walking over to her bed and taking a seat. She began transferring her belongings from one purse to the other. As she pulled out her contents, Kylee came across a picture that she and Ja'Nay had taken together on their graduation day. They both looked so happy. Kylee smiled, feeling guilty about how she'd left things with her best friend earlier. She leaned over, grabbed her cell phone and dialed Ja'Nay's number, only to have it go straight to voicemail. Deciding not to leave a message and just call back later, Kylee put her phone in her purse, turned off her stereo, and, headed downstairs to watch the episode of *Scandal* that she had DVRed a few days ago.

Kylee was all into her show when there was a knock at the door.

"Shit, niggas always wanna wait until the good part to knock on the door," she huffed, standing up from the sofa, never taking her eyes off the TV as she headed to the front door. "Who is it?"

"Who you expectin' otha than me," Eli answered.

That accent had made Kylee forget all about what was on TV. "You're the only one I'm expectin'," she said with a smile while opening the door.

"I betta be," Eli joked, stepping in the foyer.

"Whatever." Kylee laughed, catching a whiff of the CK One Shock cologne Eli was wearing.

"You look nice," Eli said, checking her out.

Kylee smiled. "Thank you and so do you." Kylee loved a man who could dress. He looked like a totally different person outside of his work uniform. Eli's locks were neatly pulled to the back into a ponytail. He wore a pair of dark denim LRG jeans that sagged just right, with a crisp white and navy blue polo shirt that revealed his protruding biceps, and a pair of light blue, navy, and white Supra Vaider tennis shoes.

"Let me grab my purse; then we can leave," Kylee said, turning to walk away.

Eli's eyes zoned in on Kylee's nice, round backside as she headed over to retrieve her purse. "You have a nice place here," he said, taking his eyes off her ass and looking around her condo. The living room was nicely decorated in red, black, white, and silver. Eli thought whoever decorated took their time with every little detail, from the red Italian leather sectional to the oversized black leather chaise in the corner with the big white ottoman that was being used as her coffee table. The authentic artwork on the wall tied everything together perfectly. He could tell there were no corners cut when it came to decorating; the room looked like it was straight out of a magazine.

"Thank you," she said, grabbing her purse off the ottoman and heading back over to where Eli stood. "Me and my mom got the idea and color scheme off a TV show we watched."

"Y'all hooked this place up," he said, shaking his head in approval.

"Thanks. Do you recognize the pictures on the walls?" she quizzed.

"Hell yeah, I recognize 'em." He smiled.

"From where?" Kylee asked, thinking he was lying.

Eli walked into the living room with Kylee close behind. "That one over there," he said, pointing, "is called *Singin' Sistahs,* that one is *Sugar Shack,* and the one in your foyer is called *Boxing Gym,* and that one over there is called *Come Sunday,*" he said, busting her bubble.

"Okay." She smiled, impressed.

"Yeah, how you like me now?" he joked, sounding like a true Jamaican.

"You know a lot about art, huh?" she asked.

"Naw, just about Ernie Barnes's work. My father had his entire collection and when he died I took 'em."

"And here I always thought that J.J. was really paintin' all them pictures on *Good Times.*" Kylee laughed.

"Wow." Eli laughed too.

"Be quiet." Kylee smiled.

"You ready?" he asked.

"I'm ready," she said, walking back into the foyer and opening the door. She waited for Eli to walk out so she could lock the door behind them. Kylee was impressed as she walked out and saw what Eli was driving.

Okay now, this nigga got taste and money, she thought as they headed down the walk.

Eli opened the passenger's side door to a stunning red two-door BMW M6 Gran Coupe. Kylee climbed in and the scent of fresh-squeezed lemons instantly tickled her nostrils. Kylee instantly fell in love with the car as she settled into the soft leather seat. Eli closed the door, walked around to the driver's side, and got in.

"A lot better than my lawn-care truck, eh?" Eli looked over at Kylee and asked with a smile before starting up the car.

"Yeah, a lot," she answered, sitting back and buckling her seat belt.

Eli pushed a couple of buttons on the dashboard and Drake's "Cameras" began playing.

"I love this song," Kylee said.

"I do too," Eli said, bobbing his head to the beat. "Where you wanna eat at?" Eli asked Kylee.

Kylee shrugged her shoulders. "It really don't matter to me. I'm down for whatever."

"I mean what do you have a taste for? Chinese, Italian, Japanese? Give me some idea what you like."

"For real I really don't care. I'm just hungry."

"Have you ever had Jamaican before?" Eli asked with a smirk.

Kylee smirked too. "Nope, but I sure would love to try some."

"A'iiiight, be careful what you ask for." Eli smiled.

"I'm a big girl. I can handle it," she said, before biting down on her bottom lip.

"That's what I'm talkin' about," Eli said, getting turned on before putting the pedal to the metal.

Kylee got comfortable, bobbing her head to the music while she and Eli got better acquainted.

Twenty minutes later, Eli pulled up in Relly's crowded parking lot, turned off the engine, and looked over at Kylee.

"You ever ate here before?"

"No," Kylee said, shaking her head. "I always wanted to try it, but every time I tried comin' here the wait was too damn long."

"That's 'cause their food is the bomb," Eli said, opening the door, getting out, and walking around to the passenger's side. He opened Kylee's door, held out his hand for her to grab, and helped her out.

A gentleman, she thought. "Thank you," she said, letting go of Eli's hand.

You could hear the Reggae music the live band was playing inside the club blaring as they headed up to the door.

"Their food gotta be the bomb," Kylee stated, looking at the long line of people waiting to get inside the restaurant.

"I'm tryin'a tell you it is."

"You sure you don't wanna go somewhere else?" Kylee suggested, not in the mood to stand in a long line.

"Naw, we good, ma, just follow me," he said, bypassing the long line of people, walking to the front of the line.

"You can't just cut in front of all these people," Kylee stated.

"Let me do this," Eli said, walking up to the dude standing at the front door. "Sup." Eli nodded before giving the man some dap.

"Sup, Eli." The man smiled, opening the door for Eli and Kylee to walk in.

"Okay," Kylee said, impressed.

From the time they walked into the crowded restaurant people treated Eli like he was some type of celebrity. It seemed like Eli gave dap to every nigga he passed by, and shot a million dollar smile at every chick who went out of their way trying to catch his attention like Kylee wasn't standing right there beside him. She wasn't the least bit bothered by these thirsty hoes. She'd never had a problem with a chick taking what belonged to her. Even though Eli technically didn't belong to Kylee, he had a top-of-the-line chick by his side, and by the looks of these females, choosing to mess with any of them over here would be a straight downgrade.

The waitress seated them at an empty table up front by the stage and handed them their menus. "My name is Chavar, and I'll be your waitress tonight." She smiled, more at Eli than Kylee.

"Chavar, eh?" Eli asked.

"Yep," she answered, slowly shaking her head.

"Give us a minute to look over the menu. But for the time being grab me some papaya juice and give my friend here . . ." He looked over at Kylee and waited.

"Let me get a glass of Cake Moscato please," Kylee answered while scanning the menu.

"What you wanna eat?" Eli asked.

"I don't know. I told you I've never eaten Jamaican food before. What should I get?"

"What you like, beef or chicken?"

"I want some beef," Kylee flirted.

"Oh yeah." Eli chuckled.

"Get ya mind out the gutta, nigga, and help me order somethin' to eat." Kylee laughed.

"Dis bully beef rice is pretty good," Eli suggested.

"What's in that?" Kylee turned up her nose and asked.

"Corned beef, onions, Jamaican pimento seeds, potatoes, spices, and rice," Eli answered.

"I think I'll pass," Kylee said. "What else would you suggest?"

"The ackee and salt fish is good, too."

"What's in that?"

"Salt fish, ackees, different spices, onions, and bacon," Eli answered.

"That sounds like a heart attack waitin' to happen," Kylee joked. "And plus, I've never even heard of salt fish or ackees."

Eli laughed. "Ackee is a fruit but it's cooked and used as a vegetable. And salt fish is just that: a salted, dried fish, usually cod. It's a meal that's usually cooked on Sundays in Jamaica. We eat it for breakfast or dinner."

"Okay, school me," Kylee said. "But it still doesn't sound like somethin' I would like."

"Don't knock it until you try it," Eli said.

"I'll pass," Kylee said, shaking her head.

"Well ya best bet is the curry chicken or jerk chicken," Eli said.

"I'll think I'll take the jerk chicken." She smiled.

"Okay, but I need to warn you, it's hot!"

"I already told you I'm a big girl," Kylee said.

"Okay, big girl, don't say I didn't warn you," he said, waving the waitress back over to them.

After placing their orders, Kylee and Eli laughed and talked as the Reggae band did their thing on the stage. Kylee was really enjoying herself. It had been awhile since she'd had this much fun.

"Now, tell me what that nigga said in the store that one day," Kylee said, before sticking a fried plantain in her mouth.

Eli covered his mouth with his fist and laughed. "Awww, ma, I thought you forgot all about that."

"Nope, and you promised you would tell me what he said," Kylee said, and waited.

"Okay, I did promise you."

"I'm waitin'."

"He said, '*Cho! Coo deh ass,*'" Eli said.

"I know that!" Kylee laughed. "But what does it mean?"

Eli laughed too. "It means, 'Wow, look at that ass,'" Eli said.

Kylee shook her head.

"What?" Eli inquired.

"I just shook my head that's all."

"My man, Jah, liked what he saw, so he spoke on it," Eli said.

Before Kylee could respond she was interrupted.

"Eli, my bwoy." Some tall, skinny guy with the same accent as Eli's walked up to the table and smiled.

"Wassup, De'lonn?" Eli smiled back while standing up and greeting him with a handshake and a shoulder pound.

"Where ya been at, bwoy? You's a hard nigga to catch up wit'," De'lonn said. He looked over at Kylee and nodded.

"I know, man. I've been workin'."

"I heard you been doin' big thangs. You workin' tonight?" De'lonn asked discreetly.

"Not right now. But I tell you what, when I get ready to leave, meet me at my car. I got a li'l somethin' I want you to test for me," Eli said.

"Dat's wassup! Fill d' splif wit' kaya and let's get higha," De'lonn said happily.

"You silly, bwoy," Eli laughed.

"I'm 'bouta go over here and wait for you by the bar. Yo de gyal ah pree mi like she waan fuck," he said, rubbing his hands together.

Kylee sat quietly with a confused look as she tried to make out De'lonn's jargon. The only word she could really make out was "fuck."

"Gwarn. Make sure you booted up," Eli said.

"No disrespect, ma," he looked over at Kylee and said. "But De'lonn goes up in nobody's ukku raw."

"I feel you," Eli agreed, giving him some dap.

"A'iiight, man, I'ma let you and ya pretty gyal get back to y'all's dinner."

"I'll see you before I leave," Eli assured him before taking his seat.

"Yep," De'lonn said before turning to walk away.

"Sorry about that," Eli said apologetically. "That's my boy, De'lonn; we both from Shamrock, Jamaica."

"It's all right. I like listenin' to y'all talk," Kylee said, enthused.

"Is dat right, eh?" Eli asked with a smile before finishing off his lukewarm meal.

"Yeah, I really do; it's kinda sexy."

"Sexy, eh?' Eli asked, smiling.

Kylee shook her head yes.

"I think you sexy," Eli stared into Kylee's eyes and said.

"Thank you," she said, looking away. This was the first time anyone had ever made Kylee lose eye contact.

"Do I make you nervous?"

"Nope," Kylee lied.

"I think I do."

"Think what you want." Kylee threw her hands up in the air and started dancing to the music that the band was playing. "They jammin'," she said, changing the subject

"Wanna dance?" Eli asked.

"Can you dance?" Kylee questioned.

"Can I?" Eli asked, standing up from his seat. "Let's go find out."

Eli grabbed Kylee by the hand and led her out on the dance floor. He began moving his body to the beat of the music. He began doing moves that Kylee had never seen. All she knew was he was rocking! Watching him dance had her wondering if he could move like that in the bedroom. One thing for sure, two for certain, he definitely had her hormones working overtime. After the fast song went off, the band started playing Prince's "Insatiable."

Eli grabbed Kylee by the waist and pulled her close to him and began slow dancing with her. The way he gyrated his manhood on her body made her chocolate cave instantly start overflowing with wetness, making her want to do some freaky things to him.

Eli smiled as he stared into Kylee's eyes as they danced. This time she stared back. He then slowly leaned in, with Kylee following suit; their lips met and their tongues did a dance of their own. The song had gone off and they were still standing in the middle of the dance floor kissing.

Eli quickly took a step back. "My bad," he said, shaking his head.

"You good," Kylee assured him, wanting more.

"Naw, ma, I betta get you home," Eli said sullenly before turning to walk away. He went and paid their bill before heading over to the bar and tapping De'lonn on his shoulder. Kylee had the waitress box up her leftovers, before grabbing her purse and following Eli and De'lonn out the door.

Kylee was confused by Eli's actions as they walked out to the car. She didn't know what was behind his sudden mood change. She thought maybe he didn't like the way she kissed, but she quickly brushed that to the side; she'd been doing it too long not to be a pro. All she could do was keep wondering what had transpired out on the dance floor that made Eli want to take her home already.

Eli unlocked the car and opened the passenger's side door for Kylee to get in. She got in and waited as he stood outside and chopped it up with De'lonn for a few minutes. He then popped the trunk, handed De'lonn a sack of his fire, lemon haze.

"Let me know what you think?" Eli said, closing his trunk.

"You know I will, bwoy," De'lonn replied.

"A'iiiight, I'm 'bouta get outta here. Holla at me," Eli said, giving his boy some pound.

"A'iiiight," De'lonn said before turning to walk away.

Eli got in the car and looked over at Kylee. "You all right?" he asked.

"I should be askin' you that question," she replied smartly.

"I'm good," he said nonchalantly as he started up the car and pulled out of the parking lot.

"You sure?" Kylee asked, confused.

"Positive," Eli assured her, and continued driving.

Kylee sat quietly as Eli talked like everything was okay. Maybe it was for him but she was still feeling some kind of way. Kylee thought maybe she was overreacting, and even thought that maybe Eli was bipolar; whatever the case, Kylee wasn't feeling it. She couldn't wait to get home, and call Ja'Nay to tell her about the disaster of a date she just had with the love of her life!

Eli pulled up in front of Kylee's house and looked over at her. "I really had a lot of fun tonight," he said, smiling.

I can't tell, she thought. "I did too. Thanks for everything."

"Can I walk you to your door?" he asked.

'Bout time this nigga came to his senses, she thought, smiling. "You sure can," she replied happily, opening up the car door and getting out. Kylee knew once she got Eli inside her house she'd be getting a taste of his Jamaican meat after all.

Eli got out of the car, leaving the engine running. Kylee knew right then the only meat she would be getting a taste of tonight would be her leftover jerk chicken. Disappointed, Kylee headed up the walk with Eli by her side.

"Thanks again," she looked at Eli and said once they made it to her front door. Kylee stuck the key in the lock and unlocked the door.

"My pleasure, ma," Eli said, smiling. "I guess I betta get goin'."

"I guess you betta," Kylee responded, not wanting to let on how pressed she really was for him to come in.

Eli wrapped his arms around Kylee and gave her a tight hug and a quick peck on the cheek. "I'll probably call you tomorrow," he said.

Fuck you mean probably? she thought angrily. "Okay," she said, forcing a smile.

"Good night," he said and turned to walk away.

"Night," she said. Kylee walked in the house, and put her leftovers in the refrigerator before heading upstairs to the bathroom to take a cold shower. After getting dressed in her PJs, Kylee climbed in the bed and called Ja'Nay, only for her not to answer again.

"I guess somebody's gettin' some dick tonight. Too bad it ain't me," she said, leaning over and turning the light off on the nightstand before punching her pillow, in an attempt to fluff it. Kylee could have easily called one of her many boy toys to get her some, but she just wasn't in the mood to mess with any of them. She wanted Eli and wanted him bad.

Kylee lay in her bed, outdone. She'd never had a man not try to sleep with her; usually she was the one saying no. Kylee tossed and turned, feeling sexually frustrated. She sat up, turned the light on, and dialed Ja'Nay's number, once again getting her voicemail. "Damn," Kylee huffed, irritated. She thought about blocking her number and calling Eli just to hear the sound of his voice. This nigga had Kylee gone and hadn't even touched her.

Kylee got up from the bed and went into the bathroom. She grabbed a bottle of Tylenol PMs out of the medicine cabinet, shook two out, turned the water on, filling up a Dixie cup, and drank them down. This would rock her to sleep tonight, she thought, as she turned off the lights and got back into bed, falling asleep within thirty minutes with thoughts of Eli still on her mind.

Chapter Nine

Nine days had passed since Kylee had seen or heard from Eli. For the life of her she still couldn't figure out what she'd done to make him give her the cold shoulder. Kylee knew it had to be something major when a different guy from Kingston's Landscaping came out to cut her and Mr. Vernon's grass. She racked her brain trying to remember if she'd said or done anything inappropriate during their dinner. Maybe she had come across too thirsty during their kiss on the dance floor. Coming up empty-handed, Kylee decided to try to let it go, but that was easier said than done. She didn't know why she was trippin' over one nigga when she had plenty others sweatin' the shit outta her! Maybe it was because none of the other ones had Eli's swag, or maybe it was because she was always used to getting her way and with Eli holding back on her it only made her want him even more.

Kylee grabbed her overnight bag. She was super excited about the romantic weekend Josh had planned for them. Kylee loved spending time with Josh. Even though he was married, he always made her feel like she was his one and only. He went out of his way to make sure she was happy. He had to in order for her to overlook the fact that he had a small dick just like Tony's.

Kylee locked the door behind her and headed down the walk. Her heart beat a hundred times a minute when she looked over and saw Eli cutting Mr. Vernon's grass. She wanted to run over and cuss him out for treating her like shit, but decided to keep it moving. She wasn't about to sweat this nigga or let him know he was under her skin. Eli threw his hand up and waved. Even though she didn't want to Kylee waved back, trying to act as if she weren't pressed, and continued on her way.

"Damn, she cold," Eli said as he watched Kylee strut to her car. His manhood jumped for joy a few times as he checked her out.

"Damn, he looks good," Kylee said, getting into her car. She took a few minutes to start up her car, hoping Eli would come over and try to say something to her. After sitting and pretend-ing for a few minutes like she was looking for something, she finally realized Eli wasn't coming over. Kylee pulled off, disappointed.

Later that night, Kylee lay in the nice, big, comfortable bed at the hotel, completely exhausted while staring up at the ceiling as Josh lay next to her snoring. Once again, she had put it down and had her victim sleeping like a newborn baby. Kylee thought about the fun-filled day she had with Josh. First he'd taken her to a day spa where they'd both gotten aromatic Salt Glow body treatments, a Swedish massage, and a Paradise manicure and pedicure along with some other treatments that Kylee enjoyed. Josh then took her on a shopping spree where he'd spent close to three grand on school clothes and shoes. Kylee had to definitely be the best dressed female on campus. Josh finished off their evening by taking Kylee to Wasabi Japanese Steakhouse for dinner, which until recently had been her favorite place to eat, that was until Eli had taken her to Relly's.

Even though Kylee had a great time with Josh, she couldn't stop thinking about Eli. It seemed like the harder she tried to get him off her mind, the more she thought about him. She couldn't understand how after only one date, he had her open like he did.

Kylee rolled over on her side and once again thought about her life and how even though she had everything she wanted, she still wasn't happy. She knew there was something missing; she just didn't know what that something was. Kylee thought long and hard about what would make her happy, coming up with nothing. Kylee drifted off into a deep sleep, only to be awakened by her vibrating cell phone. Annoyed, Kylee reached over, snatched it off the nightstand, and checked the caller ID. Not believing her eyes, Kylee blinked just to make sure her eyes weren't playing tricks on her. She quickly climbed out of bed, rushed into the bathroom, and softly closed the door behind her before answering her phone.

"Hello?" she answered in a slight whisper.

"Wassup, ma?" Eli asked hesitantly, not knowing how Kylee would react being he hadn't contacted her since their date.

"Nothin', wassup wit' you?" she asked, pretending like she wasn't happy as hell to hear from him.

"Was you 'sleep?" he asked.

"Naw, I was just lyin' here," she lied, trying to sound bright-eyed and bushy-tailed.

"Oh, okay," he said, before getting quiet.

"Did you need somethin'?" Kylee asked.

"Not really, I was just callin' to check on you, for real," Eli said.

"I been good," Kylee lied, knowing she'd been stressing not hearing from him.

"Oh, okay, that's wassup," he replied in a dismal tone.

"Are you okay?" Kylee asked, sensing something was bothering Eli.

It took Eli a few seconds to respond. "Look, ma, I know it's late and all, but I need to come over and talk to you," he said. "I got a lotta shit on my mind that I need to get off."

"Okay," Kylee responded nonchalantly.

"I got a few more things to do here at the office, and then I'll be over, a'iiight?"

"Okay," Kylee replied, before hanging up the phone.

Kylee was so hyped about Eli coming over she didn't know what to do. All she had to do was figure out how she was going to slip out of the hotel room without Josh knowing. She peeked out the bathroom door, checking to see if Josh was still asleep; seeing he was, Kylee jumped in the shower to wash away his scent. After her record-breaking shower, Kylee tiptoed over to her overnight bag and quickly got dressed in the first thing she got her hands on. She then maneuvered around the hotel room like a thief in the night gathering up all her belongings. After making sure she got everything, she looked down at Josh, who was still sleeping peacefully, and smiled before creeping out of the hotel room.

Kylee started feeling bad as she headed out to her car about how she was playing Josh. He had gone out of his way more than usual to put a smile on her face this weekend, sensing she was going through some things. She quickly got over her momentary feeling of regret once a text came through from Eli saying he was on his way.

Kylee started up her car and drove home like she was Nicole Lyons. She used every bit of horsepower her engine had to make it home in less than fifteen minutes. Thankful she didn't get pulled over by the police, Kylee pulled up in her driveway and rushed up the walk. She unlocked her front door and rushed in. She quickly ran up the stairs, taking them two at a time. She looked through her drawers and pulled out a pair of Aéropostale shorts with a matching tight-fitting T-shirt and put them on. Hearing a car pulling up, Kylee ran over to her dresser and sprayed a couple of squirts of the $150 bottle of Gypsy Water she had talked Mario into buying her. She looked down at her ashy legs and grabbed the Johnson's Baby Lotion and rubbed it all over her legs, arms, and face before heading downstairs. As soon as she got to the bottom step, Eli knocked on the door. She counted to thirty trying to catch her breath before opening it.

"I didn't think you were gon' answer," Eli said, stepping in.

"I was upstairs." Kylee smiled, before closing and locking the door. *Damn, even at two in the mornin' this nigga look good,* she thought.

Eli smiled too. "Oh, okay."

They both stood in the foyer, not knowing what to say next.

"Can I have a hug?" Eli asked, not being able to resist.

You can have more than a hug, she thought. "What you wanna hug me for?" Kylee asked playfully.

"I missed you, that's why," he admitted.

"Ummmm-huh," Kylee joked, walking into Eli's open arms.

"Damn, you smell good, ma," he said as he tightly embraced her.

"What am I supposed to smell like?" she asked flippantly.

"Just like you do right now." Eli laughed.

Kylee took a step back and laughed too. "You silly. Come on, let's go sit down," she said leading Eli into the living room.

Down boy, he thought as the sight of Kylee's firm backside had his manhood wanting to salute. He followed Kylee over to the sofa.

Kylee picked up the remote and turned on the TV. She channel surfed before stopping on HGTV.

"What you know 'bout this channel?" Eli looked over at Kylee and asked.

"Nigga, what? This is my favorite channel," she said, smiling. "This is the channel me and my mom got all our ideas to decorate from."

"This my favorite channel too," Eli replied.

"I think David Bromstad is so cute!" Kylee replied.

"What? David Bromstad is a *bumbaclot bati boy*!" Eli snapped.

"A what?" Kylee asked, laughing.

"A muthafuckin' fag!" Eli translated.

"Wowow." Kylee laughed even harder. "He is not!"

"Yeah, whateva! I don't watch shit he in. He makes me sick to ma stomach!"

"Even if he was, you act like you got somethin' against gay people."

"I do, I hate dem! That's the most disgustin' shit eva'! We don't get down like dat where I'm from and if you do, you betta keep dat shit under wraps. Or dat's ya ass!" Eli snapped seriously.

The repugnant look on Eli's face made a believer out of Kylee. "Wow, okay, well let's change the subject," Kylee said, making a mental note not to introduce Eli to Shawn.

"That's a good idea," Eli agreed.

Eli and Kylee sat quietly, watching an episode of *House Hunters*. It was killing Kylee not to ask Eli what was on his mind. She didn't want to rush him; whatever it was he would talk about it when he was ready.

"You want somethin' to drink?" Kylee asked when a commercial came on.

"What'cha got?"

"I got water and apple juice," she replied.

"Let me get some apple juice please," he said.

Kylee stood up from the sofa and headed to the kitchen to get the apple juice.

"Here you go," she said, walking back into the living room with a nice, tall glass of cold apple juice.

"Thanks, ma," Eli said, taking the glass from her hand and taking a few sips.

"No problem," she said, sitting back down beside him.

"You want some?" he asked, shoving the glass in Kylee's face.

"Naw, nigga." Kylee laughed while moving Eli's hand.

"Oh, so you don't wanna drink after me?" he teased while trying to put the glass up to Kylee's lips.

"Hell, naw. I don't know where ya lips been." Kylee smirked.

"Good, more for me," Eli said before finishing off his juice and handing Kylee the empty glass.

Kylee took the glass and placed it on the ottoman.

Eli opened his mouth real wide and yawned. "Excuse me," he said.

"You tired?" Kylee asked.

"Yeah, ma, I been up since five o'clock A.M.," he replied.

"You want me to grab you a pillow and you can stretch out on the sofa? I'll move over to the love seat," Kylee said.

"Naw, I'm good. I'm just gon' use ya legs as my pillow so you don't have to go nowhere," Eli said, turning his body to the side and lying back.

"You comfortable?" Kylee looked down at him and asked sarcastically.

"Yeah, I'm good, ma." He looked up at her with glassy eyes and responded with a smile.

Kylee picked up one of Eli's locks and sniffed it.

"My hair stink or somethin'?" he asked, smiling.

Kylee laughed. "Naw, it smells like coconut," Kylee replied, remembering smelling the same scent the first time she'd laid eyes on him that day at the gas station.

Eli lay on Kylee's lap just staring up at her. He was making her real uncomfortable, so in order to calm her nerves, she continued playing with his locks.

"What's on ya mind?" Eli asked.

"Nothin' really. I just like the way your hair feels," she replied. "What's on ya mind?"

"A lot," he said, closing his eyes and shaking his head.

"Like what?" Kylee pried, hoping he would open up.

Eli opened his eyes back up. "Look, ma, I know you been wonderin' why I've been avoidin' you and I think it's only fair that I tell you the truth," Eli started.

"Not really. I just figured you were busy or somethin'," Kylee lied.

"I have been busy. Busy tryin'a get you off my mind," Eli admitted. "But the more I tried, the more I wanted to be around you."

You too? she wanted to say. "For real?" Kylee asked, surprised.

"Yeah, ma, I really can't explain it, but I've been goin' through it. I ain't gon' lie. I have never felt this way about anybody before, especially not about a person I barely even know." He chuckled.

I feel the same way, Kylee thought. "Well if you felt like that, I don't see what the problem was wit' you callin' me," Kylee stated, confused.

Eli sat up and looked at Kylee. "I wish it was that easy. Look, Kylee, I have to tell you somethin' and I hope that you don't be mad at me after I tell you."

Kylee's heart raced as she prepared herself for the horrible news Eli was about to share with her. "Okay," she said slowly.

"Promise me," he demanded.

"I promise," Kylee said just to get him to say whatever it was he wanted to say.

Eli braced himself before speaking. He just hoped Kylee kept her word and wouldn't be mad at him after he shared his secret with her.

"I'm married," he blurted out, and waited for her to respond.

Kylee's heart sank as she stared at Eli. She didn't know what it was, but this was the first time her feelings were actually hurt knowing someone was married.

"Say somethin'," Eli said.

"What do you want me to say?" Kylee asked, puzzled and feeling jealous at the same time.

"You don't look like you'd mess around wit' a married man. I had planned on tellin' you durin' dinner, but when we kissed on the dance floor, I knew then and there I had to have you."

Nigga, if you only knew me, Kylee thought as she sat quietly and listened as Eli poured out his heart.

"I knew you wouldn't give me a chance if I told you I was married, so to spare my own feelin's I brought you home early that night. You don't know how bad I wanted to come in and make love to you when I walked you to the door, but I wanted to be real wit' you from the gate. I didn't want to build anything on a lie."

"You could have just told me, Eli," Kylee said.

"Honestly, I wanted to, ma. But that's why I'm tellin' you now. I wanted to give you the option of messin' around wit' a married man instead of forcin' it on you by lettin' you find out later on."

"I feel you, but married, Eli?" Kylee replied dramatically.

"I know, ma, but our marriage ain't what it's cracked up to be," he stated truthfully.

Kylee rolled her eyes while smacking her lips. "That's what they all say."

"I swear to you, it's not. I put that on my daughter!" Eli said in a slightly raised tone.

"Your daughter?" Kylee asked, caught off-guard.

"Yeah, ma. I got a daughter by my wife. And that's the only reason why I married her."

"Oh my goodness, not another 'I'm stayin' around for the kids' typa nigga," Kylee said, shaking her head in disgust, tired of hearing that same lie.

"That's not the case wit' me."

"What is the case then, Eli, other than you're married wit' a child?" Kylee said, trying to hide the fact that she was hurt.

"Look, I'm just gon' tell you about my marriage, or my situation as I call it," Eli said.

"Okay," Kylee replied impatiently.

"A'iiight, now look, Tionna and her girls was on vacation in Jamaica. Me and her fucked around while she was there, we exchanged numbers, and then she went home. I never even called her afterward. She was blowin' my phone up, but I never answered 'cause she meant nothin' to me; she was a piece of ass."

"Wow, a piece of ass, Eli, really?" Kylee asked, shaking her head.

"Yes, a piece of ass. Look, do you wanna hear this story or not?"

"Yeah I wanna hear it," Kylee said, shaking her head yes.

"Well, let me finish then," Eli said smartly before continuing. "Anyways, four months later she come callin', leavin' me a message tellin' me she's pregnant."

"Damn!"

"I said the same thing. I didn't believe her at first but I knew we had unprotected sex, so if she was pregnant, I knew there was a chance the baby could have been mines."

"So what happened next?" Kylee questioned.

"She convinced me the baby was mines so I stayed in contact wit' her. I flew here to Ohio at least twice a month. I went to all her doctor appointments wit' her and everything."

Kylee looked at Eli like he was stupid.

"Don't take my kindness as me bein' a gump," he said, reading Kylee's facial expression.

"I'm not," Kylee lied. "But you a good one 'cause you done all that not knowin' if the baby was really yours."

"I was raised right, that's all that is. I'd rather do the right thing while I had the chance then to regret it later on for not doing it."

"I feel you, it's just that most niggas would have waited to find out if the baby was theirs."

"Yeah, true, but I'm not cut like most niggas."

"So how did you end up marryin' her if she meant nothin' to you?" Kylee inquired, needing to know.

"First and foremost the Kingstons are very well respected in Shamrock. So in order for me not to bring shame to my family's name, I had to do the right thing and marry her, whether I wanted to or not."

"I thought they only looked down on women for havin' a baby outta wedlock," Kylee stated.

"Maybe that's the case for your family and any other family, but not for the Kingstons. It's looked down upon for women and men in our family to bear a child out of wedlock," Eli said.

"Wow," Kylee replied. "So it's your family who owns the lawn-care service you work for then?"

Eli laughed. "Naw, ma, *I* own that lawn-care service, not my family," he corrected.

Bingo! "Well excuse me," Kylee said, while playfully rolling her eyes and neck.

"You're excused." Eli smiled while imitating Kylee.

"Anyways, do you love her?" Kylee asked, changing the subject, wanting Eli to think she was more interested in hearing about his situation than his bank account.

Eli thought for a brief second before speaking. "Honestly, no, I don't love her."

"What?" Kylee asked, making sure she heard him right.

"Don't get me wrong, I care for her. She's the woman who gave birth to my firstborn, so I love her for that reason and that reason only."

"That's foul, Eli. How can you be wit' somebody you don't love?" Kylee asked, trying to hide her joy and get more info at the same time.

"No, it would only be foul if she didn't know that I didn't love her. She knows how I feel. She knew when I married her that I only did it 'cause she was pregnant."

"And she agreed to that?" Kylee asked, shocked, not believing what she was hearing.

"She didn't care if I didn't love her; shit she doesn't love me either. All she wanted was for me to marry her so she can treat me like a trophy and show me off to all her colleagues."

I can't be mad about that, Kylee thought. "This is unbelievable," Kylee said, shaking her head.

"What's so unbelievable? The fact I'm wit' a woman I don't love and who doesn't love me back? Or the fact that my wife won't give me a divorce because she doesn't want to look like a loser to her bourgeois-ass friends?"

"Man, that's crazy. Well, have you asked her for a divorce?"

"Numerous times. Her exact words were 'I refuse to let another bitch have you.'"

"That's kinda selfish and superficial, don't you think?" Kylee asked.

"That's how she cut. What can I say?"

"Well, maybe she won't leave you because of the money," Kylee said, trying to give Eli something to think about.

"Naw, ma, it's more to it than that 'cause she got her own money."

"What she do for a livin'?" Kylee asked snidely.

"She's a CFO at a huge marketing company," Eli responded.

"Damn. Well how old is she?"

Eli smiled. "Let's just say she's twenty years older than me and I'll be twenty in a few months," Eli said.

"Damn, twenty years? You got you a fuckin' cougar!" Kylee stated, surprised and a tad bit jealous of how good his wife looked for her age. "And she too damn old to be actin' the way she does."

"I guess you can call her a cougar." Eli laughed. "And I agree, she is too old to be actin' the way that she does."

Kylee was outdone by what Eli had just told her about his marriage. She knew there were some pressed and desperate older women who would do anything just to say they had a husband, but marrying a man knowing there was no love involved was unheard of.

"Can I ask you a question?" Kylee asked.

"Go ahead," Eli replied.

"Do you remember that day I saw y'all at the gas station?"

"You mean the day you were stalkin' me at the gas station?" Eli laughed.

Kylee laughed too, unaware Eli was hip to what she was doing. "Whatever, nigga!" she said, slightly embarrassed.

"Yeah, I remember. I was gon' try to holla at you, but Tionna came in the gas station and fucked all that up. I was like damn. I was hopin' I ran into you again. When you came over to Mr. Vernon's house that mornin' trippin' about my lawn mower bein' too loud, I was like today must be my lucky day." Eli smiled.

"I can't tell. I couldn't even get you to look at me," Kylee stated.

"Oh, trust me, I saw you."

Eli had Kylee blushing. Here she'd thought she was losing her sex appeal, but knowing Eli was discreetly checking her out confirmed she was still on point!

"Even though I don't love Tionna, I still don't go out my way to disrespect her. For one, we are married; and for two, I wasn't tryin'a hear her fuckin' mouth!" Eli laughed.

"Anyways," Kylee said, rolling her eyes. "Y'all didn't seem like y'all were unhappy to me. Y'all was laughin', talkin', and all over each other."

"Naw, ma, get it right, she was all over me. That was just a front. Anytime a beautiful woman is in our presence that's how she does," Eli explained.

"You really couldn't blame her when she saw this *young* tender," Kylee boasted, taking a cheap shot at his wife for being an older woman.

"Yeah, a'iiight." Eli laughed, loving Kylee's confidence. "Look, ma, it's a quarter to four. I'm about to get up outta here, but before I go, let me say this," Eli said. "I know it sounds like I'm a heartless-ass nigga, but I'm not. I can't help how I feel toward my wife. I tried to make myself love her, and thought that after Sy'onn was born it would make me fall in love with her, but it didn't."

"Sy'onn's is the name of the store I saw you in. Don't tell me you own that, too?"

"I won't tell you then." Eli smiled and winked.

Jackpot! He's not only sexy, he's sexy and got money, too. "I don't look at you any different, Eli. You can't help how you feel about a person. If you don't love her, you just don't love her," Kylee replied while shrugging her shoulders.

"I'm glad you understand." Eli smiled while standing up. "Can you walk me to the door?" Eli held out his hands for Kylee to grab.

Please don't go! Kylee thought. "What ya wife gon' say about you comin' in the house this late?" Kylee inquired while grabbing on to Eli's soft hands.

"Not shit! She don't give a fuck if I come home late or not, as long as I come. Plus, she lives in my house." Eli smiled.

"Oh, okay." Kylee smiled back as she and Eli walked to the door.

"Can I call you later on?" he asked.

"You sure can," Kylee replied.

"A'iiight, ma, sleep well," Eli said while unlocking the door.

"Thanks and you too," Kylee said, yawning.

"Man, I don't feel like drivin'." Eli spoke while yawning as he opened the door.

"You don't have to leave," Kylee said out of nowhere.

"Huh?' Eli replied, just to make sure.

"You don't have to leave," Kylee repeated with a smile, knowing Eli heard her the first time.

"You sure? I don't wanna impose."

"Impose on what? It's not like I got a man," Kylee stated, making sure she let Eli know that she was on the market.

"That's true." Eli smiled while closing the door.

"How you know I don't got a man?" Kylee asked smartly.

"Trust me, Mr. Vernon ran down your entire demo." Eli laughed.

"I shoulda known wit' his nosey ass." Kylee laughed as she turned and headed back to the living room.

"He means well," Eli said as he followed Kylee.

"Yeah, whatever," Kylee said, sitting down and picking up the remote. "What you wanna watch?"

"Nothin', I'm 'bout to go to sleep," Eli said, sitting down beside Kylee.

"Me too," she said, tryin' to get comfortable on the sofa as Eli did the same.

"Look, ma, this sofa shit ain't gon' work. I gotta sleep in a bed," Eli stated.

"That's cool; we can go upstairs, but no touchin'," Kylee said, trying to keep up the good-girl persona that had Eli fooled.

"I promise, I won't touch you unless you ask me to." Eli smiled as he stood up from the sofa and followed Kylee up to her room.

Kylee switched on the light and instantly Eli started getting comfortable. He took off his shoes and shirt before sitting on Kylee's bed and lying back.

Lord have mercy! Kylee thought. "Ummm, you not gon' sleep wit' a shirt on?" Kylee stammered, while checking out the tattoos that covered his chest, washboard abs, and muscular arms.

"What's the matter, is my body makin' you hot?" he teased while making his pecs move up and down.

Hell yeah! "Naw, nigga." Kylee laughed before turning off the light and walking around to the other side of the bed and climbing in.

Eli took two pillows and placed them beside him.

"What you doin' that for?" Kylee inquired as she climbed under the comforter.

"'Cause I don't want you to make a mistake and roll over on top of me while I'm asleep," he joked.

Kylee shook her head and smiled. "You wish."

"Good night, ma," Eli said as he turned over on his side.

"Good night, Eli," Kylee replied happily.

It didn't take long for Eli to drift off to sleep. Even though Kylee was dead tired, she couldn't fall asleep. The excitement of finally having Eli in her bed and thoughts of him being married had her wide awake. After tossing and turning and fighting the temptation to rub her hand across Eli's chest for the next half hour, Kylee finally got comfortable and drifted off to sleep, smiling.

Chapter Ten

"So you mean to tell me that you finally got this fine-ass nigga in ya bed and all y'all did was sleep?" I'reon asked as they sat around her dad's pool, sipping on strawberry daiquiris.

Kylee shook her head yes.

"Bitch, you trippin'!" Ja'Nay added. "We had to hear yo' ass cry for nine days about this nigga not callin' you. Then he finally comes over and you didn't fuck the shit outta him, wow!"

"I was not cryin'!" Kylee laughed.

"What you call it then?" I'reon asked.

"I wonder what I done to Eli to make him not call me," Ja'Nay whined, imitating Kylee.

"That nigga had this bitch over here losin' weight and shit," I'reon joked as she reached over and grabbed a blunt and lighter off of a wicker patio end table and sparked it up.

"Where yo' parents at?" Ja'Nay asked looking around.

"Bitch, I'm grown. I do what I wanna do around here, and always have," I'reon replied, before taking a long pull from the blunt.

"And that's why ya pops shipped that ass off to a boarding school way over in Spain." Kylee laughed.

"Right." Ja'Nay laughed too while waiting for I'reon to pass the blunt her way.

"Whatever," I'reon replied, playfully rolling her eyes as the smoke slowly escaped her lips. She passed the blunt over to Ja'Nay.

"Well, it's not like I didn't wanna fuck," Kylee said.

"Bitch, if you wanted to fuck you woulda," Ja'Nay said after blowing the blunt smoke out and trying to hand it to Kylee.

Kylee shook her head no. "I swear I wanted to, but for some strange reason, he got this idea that I'm a good girl," Kylee said while making quotation marks in the air.

"Where the fuck he get that idea from?" I'reon joked.

"Fa real!" Ja'Nay agreed while passing the blunt back to I'reon.

"Hell, I don't know." Kylee shrugged her shoulders. "So I just went along wit' it."

"Bitch, please, what you shoulda been doin' is showin' that nigga how big of a freak you are," I'reon said while playfully rolling her eyes.

"I know." Kylee sighed.

"So what else happened?" I'reon inquired, trying to pass the blunt back to Ja'Nay.

"I'm cool," Ja'Nay replied.

I'reon shrugged her shoulders and continued smoking.

"I told y'all everything," Kylee said, not really wanting to talk about Eli anymore because the more she did, the more the idea of him being married had her feeling sick to her stomach.

"You holdin' out on ya girls now?" I'reon asked, sensing her girl was leaving out something.

"Right! What y'all talk about? Did you cook breakfast for him? Does he snore? I mean damn, bitch, was his dick hard when he woke up this mornin'?" Ja'Nay questioned.

"Oh, my goodness!" Kylee squealed, nearly choking on her drink.

"Huh, man? I'm wit' Ja'Nay on that one." I'reon smiled while giving Ja'Nay a high five.

"Yes, we talked; no, I didn't cook; and no, he doesn't snore; and I don't know if his dick was hard when he woke up this mornin', because he woke up before I did. Now are y'all satisfied? I answered all y'all's questions!" Kylee said with a slight attitude, trying her best to hide it.

"For real for real, no, I'm not satisfied," I'reon said, before smashing the rest of the blunt out on the concrete and laying it back on the end table. "You actin' real funny about givin' us the grapes on Eli."

"I'm hip, man. She don't mind sharin' details about no other nigga she fuck wit' but we ask the bitch about Eli and she wanna get all new and shit," Ja'Nay replied.

"It's all good," I'reon said, feeling some kind of way.

"I'm not actin' funny. I told y'all everything," Kylee said.

"Yeah, okay," I'reon said, rolling her eyes.

"Look, man, I don't even know if I'm gon' fuck wit' Eli," Kylee admitted.

"Why not? Just a couple of weeks ago you was in love wit' the nigga, now you don't wanna fuck wit' him. Bitch, you bipolar." I'reon laughed.

"No, I'm not," Kylee defended herself.

"So he must really do got a gang of kids like you said, huh?" Ja'Nay asked.

"Nope," Kylee said, shaking her head no. "He only got one daughter."

"Did that nigga fart in his sleep? You know that is a huge turn-off," Ja'Nay asked.

"No, fool." Kylee laughed.

I'reon looked at Ja'Nay like she was crazy.

"What? It is," Ja'Nay said, twisting up her face as if something smelled bad.

"Anyways," I'reon said, turning her attention back to Kylee. "Well, what's the problem then?"

"He's married, that's the problem," Kylee said in a dismal tone, knowing her girls weren't going to stop with the questions until she told them the real deal.

Ja'Nay and I'reon looked at each other in disbelief before looking over at Kylee.

"Bitch, when you start carin' if a nigga was married?" I'reon asked, beating Ja'Nay to the punch.

"Right," Ja'Nay agreed.

"I don't know. I guess when Eli told me he was married," Kylee answered.

"Shit, every nigga you mess wit' is married or got a bitch," I'reon stated.

"I know, man. But when Eli told me he was married, I actually felt jealous," Kylee admitted.

"You must really like this nigga then, if you jealous of his marriage," Ja'Nay said.

"Is that what it is?" Kylee asked, unsure.

"It has to be, sis," I'reon said, smiling.

"Our girl has finally found a nigga who got her all caught up in her feelings," Ja'Nay smiled, happy for her girl.

"I'm not caught up in my feelin's." Kylee smiled, not wanting to admit that she really was.

"I'm happy for you, sis." I'reon smiled.

"Me too," Ja'Nay replied, but at the same time wishing Eli was single.

"But what am I gon' do?"

"About what?" I'reon asked.

"About his wife. He already said she wasn't gon' give him a divorce 'cause she refuse to let another bitch have him," Kylee said.

"Oh, she one of them 'if I can't have you then nobody else can' typa bitches," I'reon hissed while rolling her eyes.

"Man, from what Eli was sayin' she a crazy bitch," Kylee said. "One who's gon' always be in his life 'cause of their child. And I don't have time for no drama."

"Well, I guess we just gon' have to show her crazy ass that you not just *a* bitch; you are and always will be *the* bitch!" I'reon spat.

"Exactly." Kylee smiled.

"And plus, you will be away at college in a couple months anyways, so you and Eli can just keep y'all's shit on the low and his wife won't have to know; problem solved," I'reon said.

"That's true, too," Kylee agreed, starting to feel better about Eli's situation.

Ja'Nay sat quietly in a state of disarray. The more her girls laughed and talked about Kylee messing around with Eli behind his wife's back, the more they stirred up harsh feelings toward scheming tricks like Kylee who loved messing around with other people's men.

"Why you so quiet?" I'reon looked over at Ja'Nay and asked.

"Because, I can't believe you two scandalous-ass bitches is sitting over her plotting on this woman's husband." She frowned while shaking her head.

"Now you was just happy that ya girl found a nigga who had her caught up in her feelin's; now all of a sudden you got a big problem wit' it!"

"That was before I found out the nigga was married," Ja'Nay spat.

"Oh, so now you Ms. Goodie-Goodie, huh?" I'reon asked.

"No, but I don't make it my business goin' around messin' wit' nobody else's man, a married one at that! I think what you're doin', Kylee, is foul!"

"Who gives a fuck what you think," I'reon snapped, before Kylee could open her mouth to defend herself.

"This isn't just his woman; this man is married!" Ja'Nay reasoned.

"And?" I'reon frowned.

"Can I talk for myself?" Kylee looked over at I'reon and asked.

"Oh, my bad," I'reon apologized.

"Look, Ja'Nay, you know how I get down. You of all people know I don't give a fuck about a bitch or her feelin's," Kylee explained.

"Well, maybe you should start," Ja'Nay said, knowing the feeling of being cheated on.

"For what?" I'reon intervened again.

Kylee looked over at I'reon.

"Sorry." I'reon laughed.

"It's not like I'm tryin' to take the nigga from the bitch. I just wanna fuck him, that's all," Kylee said as if that would make it all better.

"You two bitches are pitiful." Ja'Nay grimaced.

"Bitch, don't take yo' frustrations of Quann constantly cheatin' on yo' ass out on us," Kylee spat. "You the dummy who keeps allowing him to do it!"

"I'm not takin' nothin' out on you. I just think it's foul how you constantly mess wit' these married men and don't think nothin' of it! You not gon' be satisfied until somebody plays you the same way!"

"Bitch, you blowin' my high," I'reon said, reaching over and grabbing what was left of the blunt and lit it.

"Okay, and me messin' around wit' these bitches husbands affects you in what way?" Kylee asked rhetorically.

"You just don't get it," said Ja'Nay, pulling her sunglasses down, and lying back. She began playing *Ruzzle* on her cell phone.

"I guess I don't," Kylee said.

"Anyways," I'reon said, not paying Ja'Nay any attention. "When the next time you gon' see Eli?"

"I don't know. I hope he calls me today and if he does I'm gon' invite him over," Kylee replied.

"And, bitch, if he comes over you betta let go of that good-girl bullshit and put it down!" I'reon said.

"Oh, I already planned on it. I got a few new tricks up my sleeve I've been dyin' to use, but I had to wait until I came across the right nigga. You can't just use these on any ol' nigga, fuck around, and have a stalker on ya hands." Kylee laughed.

"That's what I'm talkin' about," I'reon said, giving her a high five.

"Wow," Ja'Nay said.

"Shut up," Kylee said, smacking her lips.

"All this talk about sex got me horny as hell," I'reon said.

"Where Shawn's big ass at?" Kylee joked.

"Watch ya mouth." I'reon laughed. "She went back home last night. She'll be back in a few weeks. You know I can't stand bein' up under a nigga twenty-four-seven."

"I feel you." Kylee frowned.

"Oh, shit!" Ja'Nay screamed as she read a text message on her phone, making Kylee and I'reon jump.

"What the fuck is wrong wit' you?" Kylee frowned.

"I just got a text from Quann's boy, Teddy, and he said Quann in jail!" Ja'Nay said.

"For what?" I'reon asked, concerned.

"I don't know. I'm about to call him and see." Ja'Nay stood up from the lounger and paced back and forth as Teddy filled her in on what went down with Quann.

Kylee and I'reon waited impatiently as Ja'Nay held a conversation with Teddy. By the sound of the conversation it wasn't sounding too good.

"Okay, keep me posted," Ja'Nay said before hanging up.

"What happened?" Kylee asked as soon as Ja'Nay hung up the phone.

"Teddy said Quann let this dopefiend-ass nigga named Willie drive his car and apparently the nigga left some dope in Quann's car. Quann got pulled over, the police searched the car, and found the shit under the seat," Ja'Nay said, shaking. "I done told that nigga about lettin' them dopefiend-ass niggas drive his cars."

"Well, Quann don't got nothin' to worry about then. If it's Wilie's dope, Willie need to cop to the shit then," I'reon said.

"Teddy said he just talked to Willie before I called him and he said he was gon' go tell the prosecutor that it was his dope," Ja'Nay said.

"Let's just hope the nigga go do it. You know a nigga will say anything; that is, until the judge hang that time over his head, then it's a whole 'notha story," I'reon said.

"You right about that! Shit a nigga will tell on his own mama just to stay outta jail," Kylee said.

"I just hope the nigga keep his word," Ja'Nay said, hurt.

"Me too," Kylee said, for Ja'Nay's sake, not really caring if Quann did forever and a day.

"He got a bond?" I'reon asked.

"Yeah, fifty thousand cash," Ja'Nay replied sullenly.

"Shit, that ain't nothin'. He got money and if he don't, his niggas do," Kylee said.

"All you gotta do is get him a bail bondsman," I'reon suggested.

"True. Shit, you betta call Chuck. Chuck get all the dope boys out," Kylee said.

"Can you take me home?" Ja'Nay looked over at Kylee and asked, while trying her best to keep her composure in front of her girls. She didn't want to appear weak.

Kylee didn't hesitate. She stood up from the lounger. "Let's roll," Kylee said, feeling sorry for her girl, sensing she was trying to play hard.

"It's gon' be okay." I'reon stood up from the lounger and gave Ja'Nay a tight hug. "Call me if you need me."

"I will," Ja'Nay said, hugging her back while fighting back the tears.

"Keep me posted," I'reon hollered out as Kylee and Ja'Nay walked away.

"I will," Kylee said as she and Ja'Nay headed through the house and out to the car.

Even though Kylee didn't care too much for Quann, she kept all her negative comments to herself as Ja'Nay made several calls to Quann's boys, trying her best to gather information on how she could get him out on bond. After being told what to do, Ja'Nay sat quietly for the rest of the ride.

"Call me when you find out somethin'," Kylee said, pulling up in front of Ja'Nay's house.

"I will," Ja'Nay replied, teary-eyed, as she got out of the car.

Kylee watched as her best friend headed up the walk. She couldn't help but feel sorry for her. All the work she was putting in trying to get Quann out, and he was still gon' continue to dog her.

Ja'Nay made it to the porch, and unlocked the front door before turning around to wave good-bye. Kylee blew the horn a few times before pulling off. Ja'Nay walked in the house, headed straight to her room, lay across her bed, and cried.

Chapter Eleven

Kylee pulled up in her driveway. Her cell phone began to ring. She checked the caller ID and it was Josh calling for the hundredth time. He'd been calling her all morning. Not in the mood for any explaining, she let it go straight to voicemail. Kylee got out of the car and saw Mr. Vernon and instantly putting some pep in her step. She was not in the mood to be fooling with him either, not today. She walked up on the porch, and on one of her plant stands sat a vase with an arrangement of orange and green roses; next to that lay a big gift-wrapped box with a pretty yellow bow on it, and a smaller package was placed neatly beside it. Kylee smiled and walked over to her gifts. She had received several dozen flowers but never an arrangement quite this pretty before. She looked around before picking up the vase and putting the flowers up to her nose.

"Ummmm," she said with a smile. She set the vase back down. "I wonder who this stuff from," she said aloud, while pulling an envelope that was taped to the front of the large gift. She opened up the envelope and read the note that was inside.

The orange roses represents the desire I have to get to know you better and the green ones represents growth and life, which are two things I look forward to: growing with you for the rest of my life. I thought about you while I was out shopping, hope you like. If you do, I can't wait to see you in it and even if you don't, I still can't wait to see you in it. I need to be entertained so I'll be here to get you around seven . . . Eli

"Awwww," Kylee said, smiling. No matter if Eli meant what he said in his note or not, his words touched her heart. By far that was sweetest thing anyone had ever said to Kylee. And to have a man pick her out an outfit to wear was super sexy to her. She had a huge smile on her face as she unlocked her front door. She grabbed the large package and set it in the foyer before going back out on the porch to get her flowers and the smaller package.

"That lawn guy brought that stuff over here," Mr. Vernon said, nearly scaring Kylee half to death.

Kylee turned around and shot a dirty look at Mr. Vernon, who was now standing at the bottom of her porch stairs.

"What's his name? Eddie . . . Evan . . . Erick," Mr. Vernon rambled.

"Eli," Kylee corrected.

"Oh, yeah, Eli, that's his name."

"Do you need somethin', Mr. Vernon?" Kylee looked down at him and asked.

"What you offerin'?" Mr. Vernon asked with wide eyes.

OMG, if this man wasn't old enough to be my great-grandfather I swear I would serve his ass right on up, Kylee thought. "I don't have anything to offer. I mean you walked over here so I figured you wanted something."

"Shit, what I want from you you not gon' give me." Mr. Vernon smirked.

"You're right, I'm not!" Kylee stated harshly.

"Can't shoot a brotha for tryin'." Mr. Vernon smiled.

Kylee rolled her eyes. *I wish I could 'cause it'll be a lot of dead niggas around here, including you,* Kylee wanted to say. "Look, Mr. Vernon, I'm about to go in the house and take a nap. I'm tired," Kylee lied, just trying to get away from her neighbor.

"Had a long night last night?" Mr. Vernon pried.

"No, why you ask that?" Kylee asked, irritated, tired of Mr. Vernon being all up in her business.

"I saw that lawn truck parked over here about two o'clock this mornin' and it didn't leave until around eight."

"Okay and?" Kylee said, trying to keep from snapping.

"And I didn't hear no lawn mowers runnin'." Mr. Vernon smirked.

"What are you, Neighborhood Watch now?" Kylee asked smartly.

"All I'm sayin' is Erick damn sure wasn't cuttin' no grass that time of mornin' so he musta been tappin' that as—"

"Mr. Vernon," Kylee shouted, cutting him off. "Look, wit' all due respect, don't fuckin' worry about what goes on over here. You don't pay no bills over here and if I'm not worried about them crack whores runnin' in and out of your house all times of night, stop fuckin' worryin' about what's goin' on over here, okay?" Kylee snapped, fed up.

"I don't have anybody runnin' in and out of my house," Mr. Vernon said.

"Well even if you did, it's none of my business just like what goes on over here is none of yours!"

"Fine, I won't worry about nothin' else over here then," Mr. Vernon said, hurt, before turning to walk away.

The sad look on Mr. Vernon's face made Kylee feel bad about how she'd just spoken to him.

"Mr. Vernon," Kylee called out, deciding to do the right thing and apologize.

Mr. Vernon slowly turned back around. "Yes?" he answered slowly.

"Look, I'm sorry for cussin' at you. My parents raised me to respect my elders and I was dead wrong," she said sincerely.

"You sho'll got a way wit' words," Mr. Vernon said.

"I said I was sorry, Mr. Vernon. I had no right talkin' to you like that, even if you was *all* up in my business," Kylee said.

"I know you apologized, but I'm still hurt behind the way you spoke to me."

Oh my fuckin' goodness! "Look, Mr. Vernon, what more do you want me to do? I said I was sorry," Kylee said, perplexed.

"I can think of one thing you can do." Mr. Vernon smiled wickedly.

"Bye, Mr. Vernon." Kylee frowned while walking in the house, closing the door behind her.

Kylee couldn't do anything but shake her head and smile. She knew no matter what, Mr. Vernon was always going to try to shoot his shot.

Kylee placed her flowers on the table in the foyer before picking up her big gift and taking it in the living room. She began opening her present; she couldn't wait to see what Eli had picked out for her. She doubted if he knew her style or, better yet, her size, being that he'd never taken her shopping before. She pulled out a black fishtail pencil skirt, a red lace button-front blouse with a black fishtail jacket to match. She then ripped the paper off the smaller package, dying to see what was inside of it. She pulled the top off a pair of six-inch red peep-toe Highness Watersnake Christian Louboutins.

"Hell naw!" she said, shocked. Kylee was impressed by the outfit Eli had picked out for her. She didn't even have to sleep with him to get it and she was even more impressed he'd picked out the right size.

"We gotta be goin' to a top-of-the-line restaurant if he wants me to dress like this," Kylee said aloud as she gathered her wonderful gifts and headed upstairs.

Kylee walked in her room, tossed her gifts on the bed, and looked over at the clock. She had four hours before her date so she decided to take a quick nap so she could be refreshed and ready for whatever Eli had in mind. Kylee pulled her cell phone out of her purse, and set the alarm for five before lying across the bed. Kylee's mind wandered on what Eli had planned for the evening. Kylee really didn't care what it was; she was down for whatever. Kylee tried her hardest to go to sleep; she squeezed her eyes real tight to see if that would help, but it didn't. She even tried counting sheep, but that didn't help either. She was so excited about Eli asking her out again, she was too geeked to sleep. Kylee then climbed out of bed and looked around her room. With nothing to do until five, Kylee decided to call and check up on Ja'Nay.

"Hello?" Ja'Nay answered in an upbeat tone.

"Any news yet on Quann?"

"Yeah, I'm up here at the county wit' Teddy and Chuck now. We just waitin' on them to release him."

"Oh, okay that's good," Kylee replied, deep down wishing he could stay in jail.

"It is ain't it, girl?" Ja'Nay said, cheesing.

The sound of Ja'Nay's cheerful tone had Kylee feeling queasy. How could she be so happy about a man who constantly caused her pain? Kylee wished Quann could stay in jail long enough for Ja'Nay to get over him and move on with her life.

"Okay, girl, I got a date wit' Eli tonight. I was just callin' to check on you," Kylee said, rushing off the phone, not being able to stand Ja'Nay's good mood.

"So you really gon' go out on another date wit' Eli?" Ja'Nay questioned.

"So you really up there waitin' on a nigga to get out of jail knowin' nine times out of ten he gon' be laid up wit' another bitch tonight?" Kylee asked, going for the jugular.

"Bye, Kylee," Ja'Nay said, hanging up the phone.

"Shit, she always got somethin' to say about me and what I do. But soon as I mention the shit Quann does to her she wanna hang up," Kylee fussed as she walked over to her dresser. "If you can't take the heat stay the fuck out the kitchen!" Kylee was heated as she pulled out a pair of red lace cheeky panties with a red lace bra and tossed them over on her bed. Kylee's cell phone began to ring. She already knew it was Ja'Nay. She walked over to her bed with a serious attitude, picked up her phone, and checked to see whose number showed up.

"Shit," she snapped, seeing it was Josh. She almost didn't answer it but knew he would blow up her phone until she did. "Hello?"

"What the fuck happened to you last night?" he snapped as soon as she answered.

"Well hello to you too," she said, trying to downplay how she played him.

"Fuck a hello! I spent all that damn money on you yesterday and your ass gon' leave in the middle of the fuckin' night? And then when I wake up and call you, you send me straight to voicemail," Josh fussed.

"Well if you must know I started my period," Kylee lied, not knowing what else to say.

"Your period?" Josh asked skeptically.

"Yes, my period. You know the thing that women get once a month," she said smartly.

"Well how come you just didn't wake me up?" Josh questioned.

"You were sleepin' so peacefully and I was kinda embarrassed," she lied again.

"You still shoulda stayed. I've had my red wings for a long time now," Josh said.

Ewwww, you's a nasty muthafucka. "Well I know next time." Kylee grimaced after hearing that, doubting there would ever be a next time.

Josh thought for a brief second. "Wait a minute, last month you told me you were on your period around the twenty-third of the month and it's only the tenth. I know my wife and everyone else comes on around the same time each month!" Josh said, waiting for Kylee to explain.

Kylee lied about her period so much she couldn't keep track of what dates she gave to who. "My periods are irregular and plus you was hittin' it so good last night, you musta brought it down early," Kylee said, before twisting her lips and rolling her eyes.

"I was tearin' that shit up, wasn't I?" Josh bragged with a huge smile.

You wish. "You sure was, baby," Kylee lied. "Look, I got the cramps so I'm about to lie down and rest." She was ready to end their conversation.

"Okay, well call me when you go off your period so I can give you some more of this good lovin'."

"Okay, I will."

"Bye, baby," he cooed.

"Bye," she said, hanging up.

Kylee tossed her phone on the bed and decided to start getting ready a little early. Just as Kylee was about to head for the bathroom to shower, her cell phone began ringing again.

"Damn, what the fuck? I got a hotline jumpin' off," she said, walking over, snatching her phone off the bed. She looked at the caller ID before answering. "Hello?"

"What's up, my li'l chocolate honeycomb," Tony said.

"Hey, Tony, wassup?" she asked, annoyed.

"What you gon' get into tonight?"

"Not too much, why?"

"I'm takin' Sylvia out to dinner and after that I'm puttin' her ass on a plane."

"Where she goin'?"

"She's goin' to Florida for a couple of days to see her sister. I miss you so pack your bag. I'ma stop by the bank and I'll meet you at my house around eleven," Tony said.

As tempting as making money sounded, spending time with Eli was worth way more. "I got somethin' to do, Tony," Kylee said, walking into the bathroom.

"What you got to do?" Tony questioned.

Damn, nigga, you questionin' me like you my daddy, Kylee thought. "Me and Ja'Nay goin' out tonight if you really must know."

"Didn't you hear me say I was goin' by the bank?" Tony said, knowing flashing his money had always gotten him what he wanted.

"Yeah, I heard you," Kylee said uncaringly.

"So you really not gon' cancel your plans and come spend time wit' big daddy?"

"No, I promised Ja'Nay I would go out wit' her and I'm not gon' back out on her," Kylee said.

"Okay. Is that your final answer?" Tony asked, just to make sure.

"Yup," Kylee replied.

"Fine. Talk to you later," Tony said, hanging up before Kylee could respond.

"Fuck you too," Kylee said, laying her cell phone on the bathroom sink before getting undressed. Kylee knew she could call Tony anytime and make some money, so tonight she was going to spend her time with Eli, not knowing when she would get another chance to do so.

Kylee turned the water on in the shower and stepped in. She took her time washing her body, making sure she hit every spot twice. After showering, Kylee dried off before moisturizing her skin with some Coconut Breeze from Bath & Body Works. Being that she hadn't had a chance to get a pedicure, she made sure she moisturized her feet real good before putting on a pair of socks for extra hydration.

Kylee turned on her stereo while getting dressed; music was a good way to get her pumped for her date. Trinidad James came on and Kylee instantly got hyped as she sang along with him.

"'Gold all in my chain, gold all in my ring / Gold all in my watch, don't believe me just watch.'" Kylee walked back in the bathroom and grabbed the gel and rubbed it in all through her hair, and brushed it down to her scalp before tying it up with her scarf. Kylee sang loud and off key as Bobby Brown began singing "Rock Wit'cha."

Naturally beautiful, Kylee only applied NARS pink sherbet gloss to her lips before heading out of the bathroom and over to the bed to retrieve her skirt. She stepped into it and zipped it up on her way over to the full-length floor mirror to check out her rear view. Pleased with what she saw, Kylee continued getting dressed. Kylee then grabbed her red Giani Bernini handbag out of the closet and stuffed her phone, wallet, keys, and lip gloss inside of it. After a few last minute touches and accessorizing, Kylee sprayed on a few squirts of Jimmy Choo.

Finally, Kylee made sure her bedroom and bathroom were both on point just in case she was lucky enough to have an overnight guest. This time Kylee already had it made up in her mind that if Eli did ever stay at her house again, sleeping would be the very last thing on the agenda.

After checking herself for the fifth or sixth time, Kylee grabbed her belongings before turning off the stereo and lights and heading downstairs. Kylee was sitting on the sofa watching *Love & Hip Hop Atlanta* when her phone began ringing. She reached inside her purse, checked the caller ID, and answered it.

"Hello?" she answered with a huge smile.

"I'm on my way," Eli said.

"Okay, I'm ready," Kylee said.

"A'iiiight, be there in about ten minutes."

"Okay," Kylee said happily before pushing the end button on her phone. Kylee threw her phone back in her purse, quickly removed the scarf from around her head and rushed over to the mirror to see if her hair had lain down like she wanted it to. Loving the results of her do, she took her socks off and felt her heels to see if they were soft. Seeing that they were, she then slid her feet inside her shoes. She rushed over to the full-length mirror she had hanging in the foyer and checked herself out one last time. Giving herself a stamp of approval, she smiled and went back in the living room and sat back down on the sofa and anxiously watched the clock on the cable box.

Twenty minutes had passed and Kylee felt herself getting an attitude. Eli should have been there. Making her wait longer than she was told was absurd. Ten more minutes had passed and Kylee became furious.

"Shit, this nigga got me fucked up. I coulda been over at Tony's gettin' paid, but no, I'm sittin' here, waitin' on his stupid ass!" she fumed as she sat on the sofa, bouncing her leg. "I'ma cuss this muthafucka out when he gets here. Shit, he ain't gon' be playin' me like I'm average!"

Kylee stood up from the sofa and paced back and forth through the living room, ranting and raving.

"Fuck this shit! I'm 'bouta call this nigga and tell him I'm cool." Kylee walked over and grabbed her phone out of her purse. As soon as she was about to call Eli the doorbell rang. Kylee threw her phone back inside her purse and stormed over to the door and swung it open with a mug on her face.

"Sorry I'm late." Eli smiled while stepping in.

Kylee's demeanor quickly softened once she laid her eyes on the prize. Eli was dressed in a black Richard James blazer, with a light blue, white, and gray soft cotton Valentino shirt, and a pair of clouded-tone Levi's 513s, and he rocked a pair of black leather Gucci bamboo driving loafers. The top of his hair was twisted and pulled back in a neat ponytail while the rest of it hung loose. His cologne alone had Kylee wanting to fuck. "It's okay. I was just sittin' on the sofa watchin' TV." She smiled.

"I had to handle some business before I came over here. I stopped by my dude Big Ness house and, man, that nigga will talk yo' head off. Once he start it's hard as fuck to get his ass to shut up," Eli explained while laughing.

"How come you just didn't tell him to shut the fuck up?" Kylee laughed too.

"I tried to tell the nigga I had somethin' to do, but he just kept on talkin' like I ain't said shit." Eli laughed even harder.

"You shoulda just walked away from his ass. He woulda caught on sooner or later," Kylee joked.

"I don't know if he woulda. Anyways, enough about Big Ness. Let's talk about how good you look in that outfit I picked out." He smiled.

"I do look good, don't I?" Kylee smiled while slowly turning in a circle so Eli could see her from all angles. "And thank you for everything. I love the flowers. I never seen green and orange roses before."

"You don't have to thank me. I done it 'cause I like to see my women smile." Eli smiled.

"I'm not ya woman," Kylee said, trying to play hard while really wishing she was.

"Not yet." Eli winked.

"Ummm, let me go get my purse," Kylee said, all flustered, as she headed to the living room to get her handbag.

Eli shook his head and smiled, knowing he had Kylee off her square.

"I'm ready," Kylee said, walking back into the foyer.

Eli opened the door for Kylee to go out first. She walked out and waited for him to join her. Once he did, Kylee turned and locked the door.

"Did I tell you how good you look in that outfit?" Eli asked teasingly.

"Yes, you did." Kylee laughed.

"Oh, okay, just makin' sure." He smiled.

Kylee smiled widely. "Oh okay."

"How many niggas you know who can dress themselves and their woman?" Eli asked as they headed down the walk toward his car.

"Not many," Kylee admitted with a smile. "And again, I'm not your woman."

Kylee and Eli both looked over at Mr. Vernon, who was sitting on his porch with a couple of his buddies, sipping on a beer. They both waved. Mr. Vernon lifted his beer in the air and was about to open his mouth to say something slick as usual, but he thought about the tongue-lashing Kylee had gave to him earlier, and decided to keep his mouth closed for once.

Chapter Twelve

Kylee could tell by all the cars parked in the lot across the street from the restaurant that it had to be popular. She sat quietly as Eli pulled up to the front of the restaurant. He put the car in park and waited for the valet to come up. One attendant opened the door and helped Kylee out while another one walked around and took the keys from Eli. Kylee stepped out, fixed her clothes, and waited for Eli to walk around the car to join her.

"What's the name of the restaurant we goin' to?" Kylee asked.

"It's called Enclave," Eli said, pointing to the big sign on the front of the building.

"Oh, shit I didn't even see the sign." Kylee laughed. "What you know about this restaurant?"

"My nigga Tim owns it," he replied as he and Kylee headed to the door.

"Tim who?" Kylee asked, remembering a guy named Tim who owned a restaurant and tried to holla at her a few months ago at the carwash; but she quickly brushed him off by giving him a fake name and the number to Pizza Hut.

"You sure is nosey." Eli laughed as he checked the caller ID on his ringing cell phone.

"I might know him."

"Well if you do know him, you betta act like you don't," Eli joked.

"Whatever, nigga." Kylee laughed.

"Good evening," the doorman greeted them while opening the door.

"Good evenin'," Eli responding while pulling a twenty dollar bill out of his pocket and tipping him.

Even though Kylee was used to the finer things in life, Eli's swag had her impressed without a doubt.

"Do you have a reservation?" the maître d' asked when Kylee and Eli walked in.

"He don't need no reservation when he comes up in here," Tim came from out of nowhere and said.

Awwww shit, that is the old-ass nigga who tried to holla at me at the carwash, Kylee thought as he and Eli chopped it up. Kylee looked around the restaurant and prayed that the guy didn't remember her.

"Who is this lovely lady?" Tim inquired.

"This my friend, Kylee," he introduced.

The word "friend" stung, even though that's all she really was to him.

"Kylee? You kinda look familiar. Do we know each other from somewhere?" Tim asked, trying to remember where he knew this pretty face from.

"No, I've never seen you before now," she said, hoping they could hurry up and be seated before he remembered where he knew her from.

"Oh, okay. Well nice to meet you," he said, looking her up and down.

"Nice meetin' you too," Kylee said, forcing a fake smile.

"You know we got a jazz band playin' in here tonight," Tim said, leading them over to the table he had reserved for them.

"Who you got playin' tonight?"

"This group called S'yVelt. They bad, too," Tim said, pulling out Kylee's chair for her to sit.

"That's wassup," Eli said, before taking his seat.

"Let me know if you need anything. I'm gon' send y'all's waitress over here and go back here in the kitchen to make sure everything is copacetic."

"A'iiight, man, I will holla at you before I leave," Eli said, sticking out his hand for Tim to shake. Tim took Eli's hand, leaned down, and whispered somethin' in his ear. Eli shook his head yes. Tim shook his head and smiled before turning to walk away.

"What was that all about?" Kylee asked.

"What ya talkin' 'bout?"

"All that whisperin'. Now that's some rude shit," Kylee said, rolling her eyes.

"It would only be rude if we were talkin' about you, but since we weren't, sit over there and just look pretty," Eli teased.

"That's not hard to do." Kylee smiled.

"Hello, my name is Tena and I'll be waitin' on y'all tonight." The waitress walked over and smiled while handing them their menus.

"Thank you." Eli smiled back while taking the menu from her hand.

"Thanks." Kylee smiled, taking her menu as well.

"What can I get y'all to drink?"

"Gimme a sweet tea," Eli said, pulling his ringing cell phone out of his jacket pocket and checking the number before placing it back inside his pocket.

"Let me get a glass of Moscato. Bartenura please," Kylee said.

"Okay," the waitress said before turning to walk away.

"You like to drink, eh?"

"Not really," Kylee said. "I like to sip on Moscato while eatin' though."

"That shit too sweet for me. My wife drinks that shit too," Eli said.

No, this nigga didn't just bring up his wife while he's out on a date wit' me, Kylee thought.

"Here y'all go," the waitress said, setting their drinks down in front of them. "I'm gon' let y'all look over y'all's menus for a few more minutes and I'll be back to take your orders."

"A'iiiight," Eli said.

The waitress smiled at Eli before turning to walk away.

"It's really nice in here," Kylee said, looking around the semi-crowded restaurant.

"Yeah, he did it up. It took him awhile to get it together though. The city kept fuckin' him around wit' his permits and shit. I found out real quick that these white folks in this hick-ass town don't wanna see a nigga wit' shit!" Eli said, shaking his head in disgust. "They think all black men who try to open a business here are tied up in the dope game in some kinda way."

"That's true," Kylee agree. "But you have to admit that most of 'em are."

"Yeah, but a lot of us ain't. Majority of my money is legit. You shoulda seen how they treated me when I bought all my buildin's and shit wit' straight cash. They had the police watchin' me and everything. I got pulled over at least twice a week, hopin' they would find dope in my car. I ain't no fool. Why would I ride dirty, especially in the expensive cars I drive?"

"Wow, that's crazy," Kylee replied, amazed how crooked their city was.

"Every time they pulled me over I would just hand them my license, registration, and insurance card. And when they asked if they could search my car I would get right out and tell 'em to have at it. They would be mad when they didn't find shit. I would smile at 'em, ask 'em if they were done, and leave."

"That's a damn shame," Kylee said as she scanned the menu.

"It is. Hold on," Eli said, pulling his phone out of his pocket and answering it. "I'll be there in a few. No, I won't be there by the time Sy'onn goes to bed. Tell her Daddy love her and will see her in the mornin'."

Kylee was quite annoyed by Eli answering the phone for his wife while he was out spending time with her.

"I told you I don't know what time I'm comin' home. But I'll be there. Look, my phone is about to die. I'll call you back when I charge it," Eli said, annoyed, before turning his phone all the way off.

"Your wife?" Kylee asked, already knowing it was.

"Yep."

"You betta get home before you get in trouble." Kylee smiled sarcastically.

"I'll get there when I'm good and ready!"

"She gon' put yo' ass on punishment," Kylee teased.

"She wish she could. I'm the man."

"Whatever," Kylee said, rolling her eyes.

"Anyways, did I tell you how good you look tonight?" Eli asked, smiling.

"Yes, Eli, this is like the third time you told me." Kylee smiled widely.

"I'm just makin' sure." He smirked.

"Are you guys ready to order?" the waitress walked back over and asked.

"We sure are," Eli said, before ordering a Kobe steak cooked rare, with a salad and baked potato.

"And you?" the waitress asked, looking at Kylee.

"I'll have a porterhouse, well done, with a side of lobster bisque and a house salad."

The waitress repeated their orders before taking their menus and walking away.

"I can't believe you eat your steak rare." Kylee frowned.

"It's not all that bad. Trust me, I've eaten worse." He smirked.

Kylee shook her head and laughed. "You gotta be more careful about what you put in yo' mouth."

"Trust me, all my life I've been a picky eater. The older I get the worse I get." He winked.

"Is that so?" Kylee asked.

"That's so," Eli replied.

Kylee and Eli were laughing and talking while enjoying the smooth music the band was playing. Eli shared his future plans with Kylee and she did the same. The more they talked the more they found out how much they had in common. They were really enjoying their conversation until the waitress came with their food.

"Here are your orders," the waitress walked up to the table and said as she and another waitress placed their food down.

"Thank you," Kylee and Eli said simultaneously.

They both bowed their heads in prayer before digging in.

"This is really good," Eli said, tasting his steak. "My mother would love this."

"I remember you sayin' your father passed. Where's your mother?" Kylee asked, before blowing on a spoonful of soup, trying to cool it off.

"She's deceased too," Eli answered. "They both died in an automobile accident."

"Oh, wow, I'm sorry to hear that," Kylee said sympathetically.

"Yep, they got killed by a drunk driver. My dad died on impact, and my mother passed three days later in the hospital."

Kylee was speechless. She didn't know what to say. She couldn't imagine living life without either of her parents. Even though her dad got on her last nerve, losing him would be devastating.

"I'm sorry, Eli," was all Kylee could think to say.

"It's okay. I'm copin' wit' my loss," he said.

"How long has it been?" she asked carefully.

"Almost a year."

"You have any brothers or sisters?" Kylee asked, while cutting into her tender steak.

"Nope, I was their only child. That's how I inherited the entire estate. I got my dad's business, which my uncle is runnin', I got all their houses, and they had real nice insurance policies. I'm set for the rest of my life, but I would give it all up just to have them here wit' me," Eli said, shaking his head in disbelief.

"We can change the subject," Kylee said, sensing the pain of losing his parents was still sort of fresh.

"You good," Eli said. "Sometimes it's nice to talk about 'em. All I can say is love and respect 'em while they here 'cause when they gone, ain't no comin' back."

"You're a strong individual, because I would lose my mind if my parents passed."

"It's bound to happen, ma."

The thought of losing her parents brought tears to Kylee's eyes. "Can we talk about somethin' else, please?"

Eli shook his head yes, before sticking a forkful of salad in his mouth.

S'yVelt announced they were taking a five-minute intermission before Eli changed the subject.

"You ever been to Jamaica?" Eli looked over at Kylee and asked.

"Nope," Kylee replied, shaking her head no. "I've been to Honduras, Belize, Mexico, and the Bahamas, but never Jamaica. I would love to go though."

"I'm gon' have to take you to my country. It's a beautiful place."

"So I've heard. Do all the men there look like you?" Kylee asked.

"I'm sure they wish they did." Eli laughed.

Kylee laughed too.

After their break, Eli and Kylee both began bobbing their heads as the band started playing "Bonita Applebum."

"Tim didn't lie, this band is good," Kylee said as they began playing the Commodores's "Brick House."

Kylee was enjoying the music and the rest of her meal when she heard a man's voice behind her. "This doesn't look like Ja'Nay to me," he said, laying his hand on her shoulder.

Kylee quickly turned around and looked up while Eli went into straight territorial mode. "Oh, hey, Tony," Kylee spoke. She had been busted. She was sure Tony was going to be mad about her lying to him, but it was nothing she couldn't smooth over with some good head.

"I thought you were goin' out wit' Ja'Nay." Tony frowned.

"I was, but she chose to go out wit' her boyfriend instead," Kylee said, hoping he would buy her story.

"Oh, well how come you didn't call me and tell me that?" Tony asked.

Eli cleared his throat, feeling slightly disrespected by Tony and Kylee.

"Oh, Eli, this is my godfather, Tony. Tony, this is my friend," Kylee introduced.

Both Eli and Tony felt slightly disrespected with their titles during Kylee's introduction, but felt better knowing each other's position in her life.

"Sup," Eli replied with a head nod.

Tony nodded his head without uttering a word.

"I guess I better let you two get back to your food. You take care of my li'l chocolate chip cookie," Tony looked over at Eli and said.

"Oh, I plan on it," Eli responded snidely.

Tony leaned down and kissed Kylee on the cheek while looking at Eli, and winked. *God, please don't let Tony start no shit,* Kylee thought as Tony tried to antagonize Eli.

"Call me tomorrow," Tony said before turning to walk away.

"All right," Kylee said before turning her attention back toward Eli. "That's my dad's best friend and my best friend I'reon's dad," Kylee said, hoping Eli didn't pick up on anything between her and Tony.

"For real?" Eli asked uncaringly.

"Okay, now what was we talkin' about before we got interrupted?" Kylee said, trying to switch the subject.

"I don't remember," Eli said, with a slight attitude, but not enough to mess up his night.

"Oh yeah, we was talkin' about Jamaica," Kylee said, remembering, trying to gloss over what had just taken place with Tony showing up unexpectedly.

Eli looked over at Kylee and smiled before shaking his head. Even though he wanted to keep an attitude with her, he just couldn't. She was just too cute for him to stay mad at.

After laughing and talking while listening to the band do their thing, Eli and Kylee agreed to call it a night. He paid the bill and left the waitress a fifty dollar tip before heading out to his car.

Eli pulled up in front of Kylee's condo and looked over at her. "Thanks for entertaining me." He smiled.

"Clowns entertain," Kylee said smartly.

"Yeah, okay." Eli laughed.

"Thanks again for everything," Kylee said.

"You're more than welcome, ma. Let me get you in the house, it's gettin' late," Eli said.

Kylee hoped and prayed that Eli would turn off the engine this time before walking her to the door.

Eli turned off the engine, opened the door, and walked around to the passenger's side.

Thank you, Jesus, she thought as they headed up the walk.

Kylee quickly dug her keys out of her handbag, unlocked the door, and stepped in. Eli stepped in behind her.

"I'ma call you tomorrow, okay?" Eli said.

Kylee's heart sank. The last thing she wanted was for Eli to leave.

"Okay," she said sullenly.

"Why you sound so sad?" Eli asked.

"I don't know," Kylee said, not wanting him to know how pressed she was to sleep with him.

Eli walked over closer to Kylee. "Can I get a kiss before I go?"

"Yep," Kylee said.

Eli leaned down and kissed her on the lips. Kylee's chocolate cave instantly got wet.

"Did I tell you how good you look in that suit?" Eli asked, stepping back.

Kylee cracked up laughing. "Yes, Eli, you did, several times."

"Well, since I didn't get to see you put it on, is it okay if I can watch you take it off?" he asked jokingly.

Kylee didn't hesitate. She was not about to pass up this chance. She dropped her handbag on the floor and began getting undressed right there in the foyer.

Eli thought she was just playing at first but the more she took off the more he knew that shit was about to get real. He watched closely as she stripped off every piece of clothing she had on.

"Do I look good in my birthday suit, too?"

Eli's pipe stood stretched out like the Golden Gate Bridge. He could not believe he had one of the coldest chicks he'd ever laid eyes on standing buck-ass naked right in front of him.

"Got-damn," was all Eli could say at that point in time.

"I'll take that as a yes." She smiled.

Eli couldn't take his eyes off the cold piece of work. He scoped her out from head to toe. She was perfect in every way.

There was an awkward silence between the two. Kylee knew in order to have the night end the way she wanted it to, she had to take charge and quick. She wasn't used to being the aggressive one, but in this situation she had no choice. She grabbed Eli by the hand and led him upstairs to her bedroom and he followed with no hesitation. Once she got in the room she turned on the light.

Eli began undressing. He couldn't help himself. As much as he wanted to refrain from fucking Kylee, the head in his pants had a mind of its own. Kylee walked over and touched Eli's chest, which sent a chill down his spine. He leaned down and they began kissing like tomorrow was about to end. Their lips stayed locked as they walked over to the bed. Kylee climbed in with Eli behind her. He began kissing her neck and worked his way down her stomach and stopped. Eli sat up on his knees and looked down at Kylee.

"Turn over," he demanded.

Kylee turned over on her stomach. Eli stared down at Kylee for a brief second. He loved the tattoo of her name on her lower back. Loving the sight, Eli started at the nape of her neck and worked his way down her spine with his tongue. Kylee's body shook like she had Parkinson's. Every time his tongue made contact with her body, she shook uncontrollably. When Eli got to her lower back, he grabbed her by the waist and pulled her up on all fours. He scooted back some, took his hands and spread her legs. He planted soft kisses on her ass, one cheek at a time before his tongue worked its way to her secret garden. Kylee went berserk. She had never had a man take his time to eat her from the back. She was turned on big time. She held on to the sheets so tight, her fingers began to cramp. She tried her best to hold off on cumming, but it was no use, Eli had all the control. Eli tried to catch all her juices streaming out of her chocolate cave. Wasting no time, he flipped Kylee over on her back. He placed the head of his pipe in her opening. Eli knew what he was doing was wrong, he was a married man, but there was no turning back, not now. He was at a point of no return; he figured he might as well finish what he started. Eli still never fully entered Kylee, he just sat there staring down at her with the tip of his manhood inside of her. Kylee couldn't take it anymore; she lifted her backside off the bed, needing to feel Eli inside of her. While still in the air, Eli thrashed down, make her fall back on the bed and that was all he wrote. Eli began putting in work. Kylee was so used to putting it down in the bed, but she had nothing on Eli. She would never admit to it, but he was the best she'd ever had. Just when she was about to cum, Eli stopped and climbed out of bed.

Kylee looked at him like he was crazy.

"Come here," he said, as sweat poured down his face.

Kylee slowly climbed out of bed. She didn't know what Eli had planned, but she was ready.

Eli turned her around and bent her over before placing his package inside her warm cave. He moved a few times, before pulling her hands behind her back.

"You not about to do what I think you about to do are you?" Kylee asked.

"Just trust me," he said. Eli began fucking Kylee from the back while holding on to her wrist. Kylee had no control as he pounded her like pavement, pulling her toward him with each thrust. Kylee was loving every minute of it; she could feel every inch of him inside of her.

"Eli, I'm cummin'," she said, wanting him to let go of her wrist.

"Cum for me, baby," he said as he continued pounding her back out.

"Oh my goodness, Eli, please stop and let me cum."

"Cum, I'ma cum wit' you," he panted.

"You promise," she whined.

"I promise," he said, pounding even harder. After a few more strokes, Eli let out a roar that sounded like a lion and busted a good one all up in Kylee. Kylee squealed as she came with him.

Eli let go of Kylee's wrists, wiped the sweat from his face, and smiled at the work he'd just put in.

"Damn," Kylee said, standing upright.

"What?" he inquired.

"Nothin'," she said, worn out and completely satisfied as she walked over to the bed and climbed in.

"I put it down like a true champ, ma," Eli bragged while laughing.

Kylee closed her eyes and shook her head yes while trying to steady her breathing. "You leavin'?" she asked, hoping his answer would be no.

"Yeah, I'ma go, but I will be back tomorrow," he said.

"Okay," she said sadly.

"I'ma take a quick shower if you don't mind."

"Go ahead; the towels are in the linen closet in the bathroom. And if I'm 'sleep when you get out, can you lock the door behind you?" she asked, barely keeping her eyes open.

"I got'chu, ma." Eli smiled before walking into the bathroom.

He grabbed a towel out of the linen closet and turned the controllers on the wall and watched as the shower came on. Water shot out of three different jets. Eli stepped in and let the water from the rain shower pour down on his head as the side jets massaged his body. He couldn't believe he'd just slept with Kylee. Even though he didn't love Tionna, the entire time they'd been married he'd never cheated on her until tonight. Not that he didn't want to, he'd just never found a woman who was worth the hassle. Kylee had Eli feeling like a new man. She sparked emotions he didn't know he had.

Eli finished washing up and walked back into Kylee's bedroom. She was sound asleep. He looked down at her, shook his head, and smiled. He was really feeling Kylee. He decided to stay after all. Eli figured if he was going to get cussed out anyway for being out so late, he might as well make it worth it. He bent down and kissed her on the cheek before making his way back around to the empty side of the bed. He climbed in and pulled her close to his body before drifting off to sleep.

Chapter Thirteen

For the past three weeks Eli had been spending all of his free time with Kylee. He knew what
he was doing was wrong, and that his father
would be displeased, but since his father wasn't
around anymore, Eli chose to do what would
make him happy.

Eli was lying toward the foot of the bed, watching the Cavs vs. the Heat basketball game, when
Tionna walked in wearing a new black two-piece
panty and bra set, with a pair of six-inch stilettos.

"You like?" she asked, while modeling in front
of the TV.

"Yeah. Now will you get out from in front of
the TV?" he asked, waving her to the side. Eli
couldn't deny his wife was sexy as hell, she had
a body most forty-year-old women could only
dream about having, but he was more interested
in watching the game than having sex with her.

"This is the first time you've been home in
weeks; the least you could do is pay your wife

some attention. Can't you DVR the game?" Tionna asked as she walked over to the bed and sat down beside him.

"I'm watchin' the game, T," Eli huffed.

"Come on, Eli. Sy'onn is asleep and it's been awhile since we've fooled around," Tionna said, while rubbing Eli's back.

"Hell we could fuck all the time if you stay the fuck off the phone wit' Edna's miserable ass," Eli said, keeping his eyes glued to the TV screen.

"Edna's not miserable, she's just a little lonely, that's all," Tionna said, defending her best friend.

"Okay, call it what you want. Yessss," he cheered after LeBron made a nice three-point shot.

Tionna started planting kisses on her husband's neck. She was going to get some sex and she wasn't taking no for an answer.

"Come on, Eli, I need to cum," she begged.

"Tionna, if you don't let me watch this fuckin' game . . ." Eli frowned, pushing her off of him.

"Fuck it then!" she snapped.

"Got-damn, T, every fuckin' time I wanna watch somethin' on TV yo' ass start botherin' me. Do I come in here and bother yo' ass when you watchin' them ratchet-ass hoes on *Love and Hip Hop* or whatever that bullshit is you be watchin'?" Eli asked angrily.

"Damn, nigga, all I wanted is for my husband to fuck me; is that too much to ask for?" she huffed.

Eli rolled out of bed, grabbed Tionna by the throat and threw her back on the bed, ripping her new panties off with his free hand.

"Get the fuck off me, Eli." She squirmed, trying to get away from Eli's tight grasp.

"You said you wanted to fuck," he said, pulling his dick out of his boxers, before climbing on top of his wife.

"Stop it, Eli," she screamed.

"Shut up, bitch," he said, while ramming his manhood inside of his wife's soaking wet cave.

"Stop, Eli," she whined in ecstasy.

Eli closed his eyes and pictured himself making love to Kylee. He laid pipe like a true plumber. Tionna was enjoying every minute of it. She didn't know what had gotten into her husband, whatever it was, she loved it.

"Yes," Tionna moaned as Eli tried to blow her back out.

"You love this dick don't you?" he asked, as his mind was still stuck on Kylee.

"Yes, daddy, I love this dick," Tionna hollered as her husband pleasured her.

"I know," he said as he pulled his manhood out and came on his wife's stomach before rolling over on his back.

"Damn, nigga," was all Tionna could say as she tried to steady her breathing.

"Now can I watch the game?" Eli asked as he climbed out of bed and wiped the sweat off his forehead.

Tionna didn't reply. She watched as her husband walked into the en-suite bathroom to get himself a towel.

"Who is she?" Tionna asked from out of nowhere as she lay in her own juices.

"She who?" Eli asked, looking around the room as if someone else was in there besides them two and wiping himself down at the same time.

"The bitch you fuckin'."

"What bitch?" Eli frowned.

"Come on, Eli. You haven't fucked me like that since Jamaica. You have to have been thinkin' about her while you were fuckin' me," Tionna said, hurt.

"Look, I don't know who this *she* is," Eli said, walking back into the bathroom, wondering, while tossing the wet towel on the sink, how his wife knew his mind was on another woman. *Was it that obvious?* he thought as he walked back into the bedroom.

"Yeah, okay, you can keep actin' like you don't know," Tionna said, climbing out of bed.

"This is why I stay gone all the time! I get fuckin' tired of hearin' yo' ass bitch all the damn time!" Eli snapped defensively.

"You don't come home 'cause yo' ass don't wanna come home. It don't have shit to do wit' me!" Tionna snapped.

"Whateva, man," Eli said, while getting dressed.

"Yeah, that's right, get dressed and go on over that bitch's house," Tionna yelled.

"Man, shut the fuck up! You gon' wake Sy'onn up," Eli warned.

"I don't give a fuck!" Tionna shouted.

"Well you need to. She don't need to hear yo' ass talkin' crazy and shit. What kinda mother are you?" Eli grimaced.

"The same kind of father you are," Tionna retorted.

"Okay, T, I'm 'bouta bounce. I'll be back later on," Eli said, putting his shoes on.

"I can't do this no more, Eli. I want you gone," Tionna said calmly.

"You do know whose house this is right?" Eli asked.

"You right. Me and yo' daughter will leave. We'll go stay at a hotel. It ain't no thang," Tionna said.

"Naw, I'll go," he said, knowing he couldn't kick his wife and child out of the house he'd bought for them. Eli walked over to the closet and pulled his Nike gym bag out and began filling it up with a few of his belongings. "You really trippin', T." Eli shook his head, never expecting things to turn out like this.

"If that's the case, I shoulda tripped on ya no-good ass a long time ago," Tionna said smartly.

"I'll be back in the mornin' to take Sy'onn to daycare," Eli said as he zipped up his bag.

"Don't bother. I got Sy'onn."

Eli shook his head, threw his bag on his shoulder, and walked out of the bedroom.

"Tell ya bitch I said hi," Tionna screamed as Eli walked down the stairs.

"A'iiiight, T," Eli said.

"Tell the bitch she can have you now," she continued yelling as Eli walked out the door. Tionna looked around the room and couldn't believe what had just transpired between her and Eli. She walked out of the room and down the hallway to their daughter's room. She walked in the room, climbed in the bed with her daughter, cuddled up to her and cried herself to sleep.

Eli sat in his car, thinking what to do next. He thought about calling Kylee but decided he didn't want to burden her with his problems.

He tried calling his boy, Big Ness, but he didn't answer. So instead, Eli stopped by the drive-through, bought a papaya juice, checked in at the Hampton Inn Suites, and watched the end of the game in peace.

Chapter Fourteen

Three days had passed since Eli had moved into the hotel. He was really enjoying the peace and quiet, but eating fast food every night was getting old. He enjoyed not being around Tionna to listen to her nag and argue; it was like a breath of fresh air. Only things he missed about home was tucking his daughter in at night, seeing her waking up happy in the mornings, and dropping her off at daycare; other than that, Eli could get used to living in the hotel.

Kylee had just gotten finished with her morning run. She saw Eli's work truck parked in Mr. Vernon's driveway and smiled. She hadn't seen him since the night he stayed at her house.

"Wassup, ma?" Eli asked as Kylee walked by.

"Nothin'; what's up wit' you?" Kylee stopped and asked.

"You see it. All work and no play," Eli said, wiping the sweat from his brow.

"You act like what you doin' is hard work," Kylee teased.

"Shit, it is," Eli replied.

"Nigga, please, I could be done wit' this whole yard in less than an hour," Kylee joked.

"Yeah, okay." Eli laughed. "Why don't you come help me?"

"Help you do what?" Kylee asked with raised brows.

"Do this yard."

"You gon' pay me?" she asked.

"How much you gon' charge me?" Eli asked.

"Not much. How 'bout you take me to the Dairy Queen?"

"That's it?"

"Yeah, I told you I wasn't gon' charge you much."

"My girl." Eli smiled as he handed Kylee a pair of trimmers and walked away to finish cutting the grass.

Kylee took the trimmers and began trimming Mr. Vernon's hedges. Sweat was pouring from her face. Eli made it look easy when he was doing it, but it was harder than it looked.

Eli walked over to check on Kylee. "You fuckin' this man's shit up." Eli laughed.

"I think they look nice," Kylee said while checking out her work.

"You jokin', right?" he asked as he continued to laugh.

"No, I'm serious," she said, thinking she'd done an all right job.

"They all uneven and shit. Here let me help you." Eli walked behind Kylee and held on to the trimmers with her and guided her hands. "See, all you have to do is move nice and slow," he said, as they evened up the hedges together.

"Are we done yet?" Kylee asked, looking around the yard.

"All I gotta do is load my equipment up and we can go to the Dairy Queen."

"I ain't goin' to no Dairy Queen lookin' like this," Kylee said.

"Shit, you look a'iiiight," Eli said, checking Kylee out.

"Yeah, okay, I got weeds and shit all in my hair, my hands is dirty. And I know you ain't goin' nowhere lookin' like that are you? You got grass all over you." Kylee frowned.

"Hell yeah, this dirt comes from workin'. It ain't like I'm just dirty for no reason," Eli said, smiling.

"Well, I'm goin' in the house to shower first. I can't be seen out in public lookin' like this," Kylee said, looking down at her grass-filled tennis shoes.

"Okay, well I'ma put my equipment away, run to the room to get dressed, and I'll be back to get you," Eli said.

"What room?" Kylee asked.

"The hotel room," he replied.

"When you start stayin' in a hotel?" she asked.

"I've been there about three days," Eli said.

"I'm not understandin' why you stayin' at a hotel."

"It's a long story. One I don't even wanna get into right now," Eli said, not in the mood to discuss his situation.

"It's cool," Kylee said, respecting his wishes. Kylee really couldn't have cared less what was going on between him and his wife, and deep down she was happy they were having problems; and just maybe he would end up being hers.

"Thank you," he replied while picking up his weed eater.

"No, problem. But just know if you get tired of stayin' at the hotel, you can always come to my house and stay until you figure out what you gon' do or what you want to do," Kylee offered, knowing her father would flip his lid if he found out she had a man living in a house that he paid all the bills for.

"I don't know about that. You might get tired of a nigga and try to put me out," Eli teased.

Kylee looked Eli up and down and thought about the way he made love to her and knew she was making the right choice asking him to come stay with her. "I doubt that," she said, shaking her head no.

"I only need to stay wit' you for a few weeks. I'm 'bouta buy me another house," he said, glad Kylee had offered.

"That's cool." She smiled.

"A'iiight, I'm goin' to the hotel to get my stuff. Be ready when I get back."

"Okay," Kylee said before turning to walk away.

Eli watched as Kylee walked over to her own yard, smiled, and continued putting his equipment away. He thought back on how confined he felt ever since he'd married Tionna, but the last few weeks he'd spent with Kylee had him feeling like a nigga who had just been released from the penitentiary after serving a fifteen-year sentence. He didn't know what was so special about Kylee. He didn't know if it was because she had her head on straight and wanted something out of life or the fact that she was one of the baddest chicks he'd ever had. Whatever it was he couldn't see himself letting her go; it felt too good.

Kylee and Eli laughed and talked as they stood in the long line at the Dairy Queen. Kylee looked behind them and noticed some chick staring at her hard like she knew her from somewhere.

"You know this broad behind us who's starin' at me?" she asked Eli.

Eli turned around to see what chick Kylee was talking about. He closed his eyes and shook his head.

"Oh, you ain't speakin' now, Eli?" Edna asked.

"Sup, Edna?"

"Where's your wife, Tionna, and your daughter, Sy'onn?" Edna asked, trying to be slick.

"You don't know? I can't believe y'all ain't on the phone together," Eli said.

"No, I haven't talked to her today," Edna lied, knowing Tionna was on her way to the Dairy Queen because she'd just gotten off the phone, telling her Eli was there with another female. She could hardly wait for her best friend to get there; she wanted to see some action.

"Yeah, a'iiiight," Eli said, knowing she was lying.

"Who is she?" Edna pried while sizing Kylee up.

"Who are you?" Kylee asked smartly.

"Oh, I'm Edna. His *wife's* best friend," she said, putting emphasis on "wife" while sticking out her hand for Kylee to shake.

"I don't shake hands," Kylee said, leaving Edna hanging.

"Next," the cashier called out. Kylee stepped up to the register and placed her order.

"What you gettin'?" she looked back at Eli and asked.

"I'm good."

"That'll be $1.50," the cashier said with a smile.

Edna waited to see who was going to pay for Kylee's order so she could have something else to tell her best friend. Eli pulled a twenty dollar bill out of his pocket and handed it to the cashier. Edna's mouth flew open. She looked out the window and hoped that Tionna would hurry up. Honestly, she didn't care who he messed around with. She was just hating because it was some-one other than her. Edna had been discretely throwing herself at Eli since day one. She was still jealous because she was the one who'd met Eli first in Jamaica, but he'd ended up sleeping with Tionna because she'd gotten too drunk and passed out before she'd had the chance to break him off right.

Kylee thanked the cashier as she handed her the ice cream cone. She licked it as she and Eli headed out the door. She looked back at Edna, who was still staring at them, and smiled. Kylee watched as a black Cadillac CTS-V convertible pulled in the Dairy Queen parking lot like a lunatic.

Edna ran outside without placing her order. Eli looked at Edna and shook his head.

"Who the fuck is this bitch, Eli?" Tionna slammed the car in park, opened the door, and got out yelling all at the same time.

"Go on, Tionna," Eli said, walking up to his wife, trying to calm her down.

Edna stood beside her best friend as she went off. She looked over at Kylee and smirked.

Kylee stood in the middle of the parking lot and continued licking on her cone as Tionna screamed and cussed and Eli attempted to calm her down. She was embarrassed by how Tionna was acting. Kylee couldn't believe how this grown woman was acting out in public. All she could think about was how she wished that I'reon was there with her to see this buffoonery.

"Is that the bitch you been fuckin'? I thought you wasn't fuckin' nobody, Eli," she screamed.

"Go on home, Tionna," Eli said, grabbing her by her arms.

"I ain't goin' nowhere until you tell me what the fuck is goin' on."

"Ain't nothin' goin' on," Eli said.

Kylee's eyes bucked, but she still never opened her mouth. She couldn't believe Eli had the audacity to tell his wife there was nothing going on between them. By this time the parking lot was filled with bystanders waiting to see some action jump off.

"I can't believe you fuckin' this tired bitch," Tionna yelled as her eyes filled up with tears.

"Tired?" Kylee said aloud before snickering, glad she had cleaned up before coming to the Dairy Queen.

"Yeah, bitch, I said tired," Tionna yelled over at Kylee.

"I ain't gon' be too many more bitches," Kylee said calmly as she continued eating her ice cream.

"You gon' be as many as I call you," Tionna said, trying to get loose from Eli's grasp. "Did he tell you we just fucked the other night?" Tionna screamed, hoping to get to Kylee.

"You his wife, you're supposed to fuck," Kylee said, getting under Tionna's skin instead with her smart remark.

"Fuck you, bitch," Tionna yelled.

Fed up, Kylee walked over to the trash can and threw the remainder of her cone away before walking back into the parking lot. "Like I said, I'm not gon' be too many more bitches."

Oh, my goodness, Eli thought, knowing he wouldn't be able to control the both of them. "Get ya girl, Edna," Eli pleaded for her help.

"What you want me to do wit' her? She yo' wife." Edna smirked.

"Man, this shit is crazy!" Eli couldn't believe this shit was happening. He never wanted things to go down the way they were about to. He was heated about Edna calling Tionna. Times like this he was glad he'd never hooked up with Edna; she was too much of a shit starter for him.

"Bitch, you betta get ya life, that's all I got to say," Kylee said, as she started to get mad.

"Bitch, get ya own man," Tionna spat.

"Why do I need my own when I got yours?" Kylee antagonized her, smiling, sending Tionna over the edge.

"I'm 'bouta whoop yo' ass," Tionna said, swinging wildly, trying to get at Kylee as Eli held her back.

"Calm yo' dumb ass down." Eli frowned.

"Let her go," Kylee said.

"Bitch, you don't really want him to let me go," Tionna yelled.

"Trust me, I do."

"Go get in the car, Kylee," Eli yelled.

"I ain't goin' no-muthafuckin' where," Kylee spat angrily. "Let that bitch go. She talkin' tough. I will mop this entire parkin' lot wit' this old-ass ho!"

Eli was relieved when he saw his boy Big Ness pull in the parking lot with one of his side chicks. He jumped out of the truck and ran over to Eli.

"What's goin' on, nigga?"

"Man, these broads trippin'," Eli replied.

"Ain't shit goin' on," Tionna yelled.

"Come on, Tionna, don't do this shit in public; you too grown for this shit," Big Ness pleaded, hoping to calm her down.

"Don't say shit to me, Ness, 'cause I'm sure you knew he was fuckin' this bitch."

Big Ness looked over at Kylee. *Damn, she fine,* he thought. "I don't know shit," Big Ness said truthfully.

"The police are on their way," someone from the crowd yelled.

"Come on, Tionna, let's go," Edna said, finally speaking up, heated the action was being cut short.

"Go get in the car, Kylee," Eli said again, but this time it was in a more demanding tone.

Kylee knew Eli meant business so she listened and walked toward the car.

"I'll see you again, bitch," Tionna yelled as Kylee walked away.

"I know." She smirked while opening the door and getting in the car.

"Take yo' ass home, Tionna; the police are on their way. You know I'm dirty. I'll be over there later," Eli said between clenched teeth before quickly turning to walk away.

"Good lookin', Ness," Eli said as he hurried over to his car and got in.

"No problem," Big Ness said, jumping in his Yukon and pulling out of the parking to avoid the police himself. Eli pulled out right after Big Ness.

Tionna stood in the parking lot, embarrassed and crushed, with tears running down her cheeks. She watched as her husband pulled off with another chick in his car, never once looking back at her.

Chapter Fifteen

"You cool?" Eli looked over at Kylee and asked as he weaved in and out of traffic, trying to get as far away from the Dairy Queen as possible.

"I'm good," she said with an attitude.

"Look, I didn't mean for shit to go down like that. I shoulda known Edna's miserable ass was gon' call Tionna."

"Life is full of surprises," Kylee replied as she stared out the window. Kylee sat quietly as Eli continued to drive.

"Why you so quiet?" Eli asked.

"I'm just thinkin', that's all," she answered.

"About?"

"The bullshit that just went down between me and yo' wife. That's the type of shit that could get a muthafucka fucked up." Kylee frowned.

"I know, ma, and I'm sorry."

"Did you just fuck her the other day?" Kylee asked, looking out the window, wanting to know; not that it was going to change anything, she just wanted to know.

Eli looked over at Kylee and didn't know if he should tell the truth, but he didn't want to lie to her. "Yeah, I fucked her," he answered and sat quietly for a brief minute while Kylee let the news sink in. "You mad at me now?"

"Mad for what?" Kylee asked as her blood boiled. She knew Tionna had the right to come to the Dairy Queen and trip like she did. "Like I said, she is yo' wife."

"I don't know what to say, ma," Eli said.

"You said enough," Kylee replied, trying to fight back her tears. She didn't know why finding out Eli had slept with his wife bothered her so much. It must have been the thought of him sleeping with someone other than her. She said it herself: Tionna was his wife.

Eli pulled up in front of Kylee's house and shut the engine off. "Now what?" he looked over at her and asked.

"What do you mean?"

"What we gon' do?" he asked.

"I don't know about you, but I'm goin' in the house. It's hot as hell out here," Kylee said, getting out of the car.

Eli got out too and followed Kylee up the walk.

"You not gon' get yo' clothes out the car?" she asked, still mad. Kylee was upset but not enough to send him back to the hotel.

"Shit, I didn't know if you still wanted me here," Eli said.

"If I didn't want you here, you wouldn't be," Kylee said as she walked up on the porch.

Eli walked back to the car to get his gym bag out of the trunk, happy Kylee still wanted him there with her. As he headed back up the walk an Edible Arrangements truck pulled up in Kylee's driveway. He looked at the driver like he had the wrong address. The driver got out of the truck, carrying a huge confetti fruit cupcake with a wide variety of fruits, chocolates, and gourmet white chocolate–dipped strawberries, and bananas.

"Who you lookin' for, homey?" Eli asked the driver while walking up on the porch.

The driver pulled the card from the top of the arrangement and read it. "Kylee Hampton. Does she live here?"

"Yeah. Eh, Kylee you got a delivery out here," Eli yelled through the screen door.

"Huh? I didn't hear you," Kylee said, walking out on the porch, smiling when she saw the delivery guy.

"Kylee Hampton?" the driver asked.

"That be me." She smiled, taking the huge arrangement from the delivery guy.

"You have a nice day," the driver said, walking back toward his truck.

"This is so sweet." Kylee smiled while heading back into the house.

"Who sent that?" Eli asked, dropping his gym bag down and following Kylee into the kitchen.

"I don't know," she said, pulling the card from the stick and reading it. She smiled when she saw that it was from Antoine. It had been awhile since she heard from him.

"Who it's from?" Eli asked again while laying his cell phone on the counter.

"Nigga, you got a lot of nerve to be questionin' me. Did you forget you're a married man?" Kylee said before pulling a strawberry off and sticking it in her mouth.

"You right." Eli laughed, not because something was funny, but to keep himself from flipping.

"If you really must know it's from my friend, Antoine," she said, popping a grape in her mouth.

"Antoine, eh?" he asked, not really feeling Kylee having male friends, even though he was married.

"Yeah, Antoine. You want some?" she asked, grabbing another strawberry, attempting to hand it to Eli.

"Hell naw, I don't want none of that bullshit." He frowned before walking out of the kitchen, leaving Kylee alone to indulge in her scrumptious gift. Eli grabbed his bag and headed upstairs. He wasn't feeling another nigga sending Kylee gifts. He knew he couldn't do anything at this point in time but accept what Kylee had said and deal with it. He unzipped his bag, pulled out his hygiene bag, basketball shorts, and a pair of boxers before heading to the shower. All Eli could think about as the hot water massaged his tense body was he hoped he had made the right choice by leaving Tionna and moving in with Kylee for the time being. After showering, Eli brushed his teeth, rubbed himself down with baby oil, and sprayed some coconut oil in his head before walking back into the bedroom.

"You okay up . . ." Kylee asked, walking into the bedroom, stopping in midsentence when she saw Eli lying on the bed with his shirt off.

"Yeah, I'm good. Just got out the shower. I don't know what you want me to do wit' my dirty clothes, so I just left 'em in the bathroom."

"On the floor, nigga?" Kylee grimaced. "You know that little small room that's off the kitchen? I don't know what y'all call 'em in Shamrock, but us over here in America call 'em laundry rooms."

"A'iiiight, smart ass." Eli laughed. "Come here," Eli said.

"What you want?" Kylee asked, smiling.

"Come see."

Kylee couldn't resist. She walked over to the bed and stood over Eli. "What?" she asked, with her hands on her hips.

Eli stood up and looked Kylee in her eyes and with a serious look on his face he said, "Don't make me regret this."

"I won't," she replied, not questioning what he meant because she already knew.

"What we gon' do about all your male friends?" he asked.

"The same thing we gon' do about Tionna," she replied.

"What's that?" he asked.

"Deal wit' it," she said smartly.

"A'iiiight, smart ass. Don't make me fuck you up." Eli laughed while grabbing Kylee by the waist, pulling her into his space, and began kissing her on her neck.

"Don't start nothin' you ain't gon' finish," Kylee said, laying her head back as Eli planted soft kisses all over her neck and shoulders. Kylee felt Eli's dick poke her through his shorts.

"You want this?" he asked, grabbing himself.

"Yep," Kylee smiled.

"You gon' fuck my face?" he asked, before hitting her with the LL Cool J lip lick.

Kylee instantly got turned on. "You want me to?" she asked.

"Yep."

Kylee slowly got undressed as Eli watched her. She climbed in the bed, lying on her back and motioning Eli to come to her. Eli removed his shorts and boxers before climbing in the bed. He didn't waste any time diving into her sugar bowl. Kylee wrapped her long legs around Eli's neck as he ate her like he was at an all-you-can-eat buffet.

"Eli," she moaned as she lifted her ass off the bed, trying to get Eli's tongue to go deeper inside of her.

Eli was so engrossed in pleasing Kylee he didn't respond.

"Oh, my god!" Kylee screamed out as her juices exploded and ran down Eli's face. Her body shook as Eli guided his manhood into her dripping wet walls.

"You ready for this?" He looked down at Kylee and asked as he guided his manhood into her dripping wet walls.

"Yes," she said in an almost begging manner.

Eli gave Kylee what she wanted. He made love to her for the next forty-five minutes, making her cum twice before cumming himself.

"You satisfied?" he asked, rolling over on his back.

Kylee shook her head yes.

"Good. I'm 'bouta take a nap. I want somethin' to eat when I wake up," Eli said jokingly as he pulled the comforter up over him.

"Shit, nigga, you just ate. You didn't get full?" Kylee joked.

"Whateva." Eli laughed.

"I'll cook you somethin' when I get out the shower," Kylee said, climbing out of the bed and heading toward the bathroom.

"Good lookin'," Eli said while yawning.

Kylee took a quick shower and got dressed before going down to the kitchen to see what she could fix Eli to eat. She was on cloud nine as she looked in the bare refrigerator. She was so happy Eli had decided to move in with her temporarily, but if his sex game was that good all the time, he could stay forever. Finding nothing to eat, Kylee decided to order Chinese.

As Kylee was flipping through the pages of the phone book to find Hong Kong Fuey's phone number, she heard a vibrating noise. She looked under the phone book and saw that it was Eli's cell phone. She picked up the phone and checked the caller ID. Her heart raced when the name came across as T. If she remembered right, she'd heard Eli calling Tionna "T" a few times at the Dairy Queen.

Kylee wanted to answer his phone so bad she could taste it. Whoever this T person was they desperately wanted to talk to Eli because every time the phone stopped vibrating they would call right back. The temptation was too great. Kylee was nervous as she pushed the talk button.

"Hello?" she answered as her stomach filled up with butterflies.

"Hello?" Tionna asked with serious attitude.

Kylee quickly recognized her voice. "Yes," Kylee sang.

"Who is this?" Tionna asked.

"You already know who this is, don't play stupid," Kylee said.

"Yeah whatever. Put Eli on the phone, bitch," Tionna spat.

I told this old trick about that bitch word, Kylee thought. "He's asleep. I would wake him, but he looks so peaceful with my dried pussy juice all around his mouth," Kylee retorted.

"Bitch, I'ma kill you," Tionna screamed into the receiver. "I swear on my daughter."

Kylee started laughing. "You shouldn't swear on your daughter, it's tacky. I'll tell Eli to call you when he wakes up," Kylee said, pushing the end button as Tionna continued making threats.

As Kylee placed their orders for their Chinese food, Eli's phone went off at least twenty more times. She couldn't believe how many times Tionna had called back

"Desperate bitch," Kylee said, shaking her head while erasing all of Tionna's calls before walking into the living room to wait for their order.

Eli woke up from his nap and came downstairs just as Kylee finished fixing their plates.

"Ummm, somethin' smells good," he said, walking into the kitchen. He walked behind Kylee, wrapped his arms around her waist, and kissed her neck.

"Here go my phone. I was lookin' for this," he said, picking it up and checking his missed calls.

"Did you sleep good?" she asked.

"Huh?" he asked, not catching what she'd said because he was too busy trying to read the numerous text messages from Tionna.

"I said did you sleep good?" she repeated nervously, hoping Tionna didn't bust her out for answering his phone.

Too much for him to read, Eli shook his head before laying the phone back down on the counter. "Yep, I slept good."

"That's good." She smiled. "I need to go to the grocery store, so I just ordered a variety of

Chinese food," she said, setting his plate down on the table.

"That's wassup." He smiled, sitting down at the table and bowing his head in prayer before eating. "The game about to come on," Eli said, looking at the clock on the microwave.

"Who's playin'?" Kylee asked, even though she could not have cared less.

"The sorry-ass Lakers and the Celtics. It's gon' be a good-ass game," Eli said.

"Well go watch it," Kylee suggested.

"Say what?" Eli asked, surprised.

"Go watch the game." Kylee laughed.

Eli wasn't used to a woman telling him to watch basketball. "You not gon' be botherin' me are you?" he asked.

"You got my word. I will not bother you while your game is on." Kylee smiled.

"Cool," Eli said, sounding like a big kid. He picked up his plate, grabbed a bottle of water out of the refrigerator, and headed upstairs to watch the game.

Kylee's cell phone began to ring as she sat at the kitchen table, finishing off her food. She checked the number before pressing the talk button.

"Sup?" she answered.

"What you doin'?" Ja'Nay asked.

"Nothin', sittin' here eatin', what's up?" Kylee asked.

"Did you do your paperwork for housin'? You know it's due next week. And did you finish your FAFSA?" Ja'Nay asked.

"Oh, shit!" Kylee snapped. She was so occupied with Eli it had totally slipped her mind to take care of all the paperwork that should have been completed weeks ago.

"That's a damn shame! We gon' fuck around and get the leftover rooms," Ja'Nay said.

"Well how come you didn't remind me?" Kylee said, trying to blame Ja'Nay for her own mistakes.

"Well, I'm remindin' you now. Get your shit done tomorrow so we can get the fuck up outta Ohio," Ja'Nay said, ready to leave.

"I can't believe you really gon' leave Quann's ass," Kylee said, impressed.

"Girl, I ain't thinkin' about Quann's ass. I heard he fuckin' some bitch named Trenity who lives over on the north," Ja'Nay said, shaking her head, knowing she should be used to Quann's cheating ass.

"Are you surprised?"

"Not at all." Ja'Nay sighed. "I just hope that bitch hold him down when he go turn himself in to do them two years he's facin'."

"What? I thought that dopefiend told the prosecutors the dope belonged to him," Kylee stated.

"Girl, he did. That was until they told his ass he was goin' to jail; then his ass recanted his story and started singin' like Jodeci. He told 'em everything," Ja'Nay said.

"See, I told you niggas will tell on their own mama."

"You did say it. Oh well, finish eatin'."

"Okay, call me if you need to talk," Kylee said, feeling bad for her friend, knowing she was hurt even though she was mad at Quann for the moment. With the right choice of words, Ja'Nay would be right back in Quann's corner just like always.

"Okay, I will, and don't forget to get all your paperwork turned in tomorrow," Ja'Nay said.

"I got'chu," Kylee assured her.

"All right. Oh, before I go, I'reon said we goin' to the mall tomorrow around one," Ja'Nay said.

"Oh, okay, cool," Kylee said. It had been a minute since she'd hung out with her friends; going to the mall was something she was looking forward to doing.

"Talk to you later," Ja'Nay said before hanging up.

Kylee finished up her meal and cleaned up the kitchen before going upstairs to watch the game with Eli.

Chapter Sixteen

Kylee woke up the next morning and rolled over to an empty bed. She wiped her eyes before looking over at the clock. It was past eleven o'clock when she woke up. Eli was really wearing her out. After the game went off the night before, Eli rewarded Kylee with some more good loving for not pestering him while the game was on. She climbed her sore, naked body out of bed and headed downstairs to get something to drink. Lying on the counter was a note and a stack of money. Kylee picked the note up and read it.

Here is some grocery money and money for rent and bills. I'll see you when I get off work.
Love, Eli

"Love?" Kylee held the letter up to her chest. "I love you too." She smiled happily before picking the money up and counting it. "A thousand dollars, wow. And I didn't have to do some foul shit to get it."

Kylee poured herself a glass of orange juice before heading back upstairs to get dressed so she could meet her girls at the mall. After deciding on a simple yellow Tommy Girl polo tee, a pair of Roxy jean shorts, and some Roxy flip-flops, Kylee headed to the bathroom to shower. After getting dressed, she was ready to meet up with her girls. She called Ja'Nay and told her to be ready. Kylee grabbed her brown and yellow cross-body Dooney & Bourke satchel and headed out the door. She was surprised to see her car shining like new money. Eli must have detailed it while she was asleep. Kylee smiled and headed down the walk.

"Eli took your car to the carwash this mornin'," Mr. Vernon yelled from his front porch. "He done a good job, didn't he?"

Kylee came to terms that, no matter what, Mr. Vernon was never going to mind his business. She just had to suck it up and deal with it.

"He sure did," Kylee said happily, hitting the unlock button on her keychain. The scent of fresh linen poured out when she opened the car door.

Kylee started up the car and pulled off. She turned to an old-school station on the satellite radio. She began dancing in her seat as Foxy Brown's "Get Me Home" came on. The music had Kylee in a zone and she didn't even realize she'd started speeding. Without warning a police car pulled out from behind a billboard.

"Shit," Kylee said, seeing the flashing lights in her rearview mirror. Kylee pulled over to the side of the road. She was glad to see that it was a man instead of woman getting out of the cruiser. The women always gave her a ticket; she could always play the damsel in distress when it came to the men. Kylee quickly pulled her shirt so her cleavage could be seen and pulled her shorts up, showing her thighs. The tall, dark officer walked up to the passenger's side of the car.

"What's the problem, Officer?" Kylee asked, rolling down the window.

"Do you know how fast you were goin'?" he asked sternly.

"Honestly, no, I don't. Was I speedin'?" she asked, batting her eyes.

"You were doin' fifty in a twenty-five," he stated.

"I was?" Kylee asked, surprised, thinking she was going much faster than that.

"Yes, you were," the officer replied. "License and registration."

"Ummm, what's your name?" Kylee asked.

"Officer is good enough," he stated smartly.

This was not going to be as easy as Kylee thought. This guy was a straight prick. She had to think fast to get herself out of this ticket.

"I really didn't know I was speedin'," she said, digging in her purse, handing him her license. "I just caught my boyfriend in bed wit' my best friend and now I don't know what I'm gon' do. It's his house and I have no place to go." Tears filled Kylee's eyes as she leaned over and pulled her registration out of the glove compartment, handing it to the officer. "I have no family here. I'm fucked!"

"Sorry to hear that," the officer said as his demeanor softened. "You eighteen, huh?" the officer asked, looking at Kylee's birth date on her license.

"Yes." She sniffed.

"You can always go stay in a shelter until you find somewhere to go."

"I'll probably just sleep in my car," Kylee said.

"It's too dangerous for a pretty little lady like you to sleep in yo' car," the officer said.

"Well, what am I supposed to do?" Kylee asked as the fake tears flowed.

The officer's eyes zoned in on Kylee's ta-tas as he spoke. "Look, I normally wouldn't do this. But you seem nice enough. Why don't you meet me at my house and we will try to see what we can come up with?" he offered.

"You would do that for me?" Kylee asked happily.

"Yeah, but you have to keep it between us," he said.

"I won't tell anybody, I promise." Kylee smiled.

"Let me write down my address. I get off work at five, just meet me there," he said, handing Kylee's license and registration back.

"Wow, you are so nice," Kylee said.

"That's what I'm here for, to protect and serve," he replied with more than just doing his job on his mind. The officer pulled out his ticket book and wrote his address on the back of one of the tickets and handed it to Kylee.

"You said five right?" Kylee asked, taking the piece of paper from his hand.

"Yep. Five," he answered.

"So what am I supposed to do until then? I don't have nowhere to go or nothin' to do," she said.

The officer pulled his wallet out of his back pocket, opened it up, and handed Kylee a fifty dollar bill. "Take yourself to lunch and a movie," he said.

Kylee took the money from his hand. "Wow, thank you so much."

"No problem. Okay, I have to go. I got another call comin' in and I'll see you at five," the officer said, tipping his hat.

"I can't wait." Kylee smiled, biting down on her bottom lip and hitting him with the sexy drunk look.

The officer's dick started to get hard. "And I can't either." He smirked.

I'ma fuck the shit outta that young bitch, then put her out my house, the officer thought anxiously as he walked away.

Kylee watched as the officer walked back to his cruiser and got in. He smiled and blew the horn as he drove past her.

Kylee smiled and waved back before balling up his address and tossing it out the window. "Dumb ass," she said, pulling off.

Kylee and Ja'Nay laughed about how Kylee played the officer as they pulled up in the mall's parking lot.

"Bitch, I gotta give it to you, you got a cold mouthpiece," Ja'Nay said, giving her girl props.

"I do don't I?" Kylee agreed.

Kylee and Ja'Nay got out of the car and headed into the mall. They spotted I'reon sitting in the food court, talking on her cell phone. I'reon smiled and waved as they walked toward her.

"*Te extrano,*" I'reon cooed.

"She must be talkin' to Enrique Iglesias," Kylee joked.

I'reon made a funny face at Kylee and Ja'Nay. "*Si, te amo. Adios,*" I'reon said, hanging up her phone.

"You need to cut all that lovey-dovey gay shit out," Kylee joked, taking a seat at the table.

"Oh, bitch, you got a lotta nerve. As much as I gotta hear about Eli and how he be puttin' in work." I'reon laughed.

"Who you tellin'," Ja'Nay said, taking a seat as well.

"Do I really talk about Eli a lot?" Kylee asked, not aware of how much she really did talk about Eli to her girls.

"Yes," Ja'Nay and I'reon said simultaneously.

"Oh, my bad." Kylee laughed.

"It's okay, girl, as long as you happy," I'reon said sincerely.

"Bitch, you bet' not open yo' mouth," Kylee said, looking over at Ja'Nay before she could open her mouth to talk about how wrong she was for messing with a married man.

Ja'Nay threw her hands up. "Hey, I don't got shit to say. If you like it, I love it," she said.

"Good. Now let's go spend some money." Kylee laughed.

"Wait, I got somethin' to tell y'all," I'reon said, smiling.

"Is it good news or bad news?" Ja'Nay asked.

"It's good news; well, at least it is for me," she replied.

"Let me guess. You pregnant by Shawn. Oh, wait, that's impossible being that she's a bitch too," Kylee joked.

Ja'Nay and I'reon both laughed.

"Whatever, heffa," I'reon said. "Anyways, no, I'm not pregnant."

"Well what's the good news?" Ja'Nay asked.

"I'm movin'," I'reon blurted out.

"Where you movin' to? Let me decorate for you," Kylee said, smiling.

"I would love for you to decorate my place for me. Are you willin' to fly to Spain to do so?" I'reon asked.

"Spain?" Ja'Nay asked, surprised.

"Spain?" Kylee repeated, surprised as well.

"Yes, Spain," I'reon replied.

"Wait a minute, bitch. You movin' back to Spain?" Kylee asked again, just to make sure she heard right.

"Yes." I'reon smiled.

"Why?" Kylee asked.

"Shawn doesn't like America. She can't adjust to our ways."

"So you willin' to just pick up and leave your family for a piece of pussy?" Kylee asked, thinking about how it sounded after saying it.

Ja'Nay and I'reon both frowned.

"I know, that didn't sound right, did it?" Kylee asked, laughing.

"No, it sounded nasty." I'reon laughed too.

"Well, it's the truth," Kylee said.

"True," Ja'Nay added.

"I can't believe you're leavin' 'cause Shawn can't adjust to our ways. It's a million illegal immigrants over here in America. Just call a 1-800 number and you'll see what the fuck I'm talkin' about," Kylee said, not feeling the fact that her god-sister was leaving her again, but this time it was by choice.

I'reon and Ja'Nay laughed.

"So when you leavin'?" Kylee asked, hurt, but trying not to show it.

"Next week," I'reon replied.

"Next week?" Ja'Nay and Kylee both shouted.

"Shhhhh." I'reon laughed, looking around.

"Why so soon?" Kylee asked.

"'Cause I miss Shawn."

"You must really like this broad," Kylee said, shaking her head, still not able to grasp the fact that her god-sister was in love with a woman.

"I do love Shawn. It ain't no different than bein' in love wit' a man," I'reon stated.

"There's a big difference. A man is born wit' a dick; no matter how big or small, he still came into the world wit' it. Shawn has to strap hers on," Kylee stated smartly.

I'reon and Ja'Nay laughed.

"You so nasty." I'reon smiled.

"What did your parents say about all this?" Ja'Nay asked.

"They both think me goin' back to Spain is a good idea," I'reon replied. "And just think, if I get homesick, I can always come back."

"Yeah, true," Ja'Nay said.

"I'll be home every holiday and y'all can fly over to see me on spring break and during the summer," I'reon said.

"That's true," Kylee agreed, still not feeling the news of I'reon moving, but trying to sound supportive at the same time.

I'reon stood up from her chair. "Y'all ready to go spend some money?"

"You know I am," Kylee said, throwing her satchel strap over her body and standing up too.

"Let's do this," Ja'Nay said, standing up.

The three friends walked out of the food court laughing and talking like old times. Kylee knew she had to get used to I'reon being gone all over again. She just hoped it didn't hurt as bad as the first time had. Knowing she had Eli to help occupy her time might make I'reon leaving again much easier.

Chapter Seventeen

Kylee was awakened by someone banging on the door like the police. She jumped up, looked over at the clock, and instantly got mad.

"Who the hell beatin' on my door at nine o'clock in the mornin'?" she yelled angrily as she headed downstairs to answer the door.

"It's your father," he answered.

What the fuck you want this early? she thought, swinging the door open with a mug on her face.

"What the fuck is this?" her dad walked in the house yelling while shoving a piece of paper in Kylee's face.

"I don't know," she said, snatching it from his hand and reading it.

"What do you have to say for yourself?" her father asked, angrily waiting for her to read the letter.

"I forgot," she replied slowly.

"How in the hell did you forget to apply for housing and your FAFSA?" her dad scolded her. "What the fuck you been doin' the entire summer? You've had plenty of time to get all of this shit taken care of, Kylee!"

Kylee stood quietly as her dad went ham.

"You know what this means? It means you're not goin' to college in the fall! 'Cause you don't have a place to stay nor do you have financial aid," her father hollered. "I could pay for your tuition, but I'm not. It's time for you to grow the fuck up and learn some responsibility."

"I'll just go winter quarter," Kylee said, hoping that would make her dad happy.

"Did you at least do Ja'Nay's paperwork like you promised her you would?" he asked.

"No," Kylee answered slowly.

"What! You not only fuckin' up your own future, you fuckin' up Ja'Nay's, too."

"I said I forgot, dang!" Kylee huffed.

"You forgot is all you can come up with?" her father asked, disgusted.

Kylee didn't answer. She didn't have any other explanation. She'd told him the truth. She really did forget to do their paperwork. She sure wasn't going to tell him about Eli. Her mind had been so occupied playing house with Eli, she'd completely let her dad and Ja'Nay down.

"Who shoes are these?" her dad asked, looking down at the men's tennis shoes that were stacked neatly against the wall in the foyer.

Oh shit! Kylee thought, forgetting they were there. Things were about to get real ugly.

"You got a nigga livin' up in here?" her dad asked.

"He just stayin' here until he buy him a house," Kylee said.

"I can't believe this shit! First, you fuck up your chances of goin' to college; then you move a nigga up in some shit I pay for, knowin' I wouldn't approve of it." Her father chuckled out of anger.

"He's about to buy him a house. He only gon' be here a few more weeks," Kylee said, hoping that made things better.

Kylee's father looked at her like she was crazy. "I wouldn't give a damn if he was about to buy two houses! Look, Kylee, I love you and you grown and I'm about to start treatin' you as such. I don't know how you gon' pay your bills but you betta figure somethin' out."

"That's fine," Kylee retorted.

Kylee's father looked at his only child and shook his head before storming back out the door. Kylee knew her father was disappointed in her, which was the last thing she wanted. But he was right: she was grown, and forgetting to handle her and Ja'Nay's business was something she was going to have to deal with, not him.

Kylee walked back upstairs and hurried into her room to answer her ringing cell phone. She looked at the number and shook her head.

"Hello?" Kylee answered.

"So I guess we don't get to go to college," Ja'Nay said, holding the letter she'd just received in the mail.

"I'm so sorry, Ja'Nay," Kylee said sincerely. "We can always go for the winter quarter."

"Winter quarter? What the fuck am I gon' do now? My mom said if I don't go to college I gotta get a job to help out around the house. Shit, my mom don't got money like yours and I'reon's." Ja'Nay was crushed. "I wished I would have just done my own paperwork like I started to, and I wouldn't be in this predicament now."

"I said I was sorry, damn!"

"I gotta go," Ja'Nay said, hanging up.

"Damn, why everybody mad at me?" Kylee asked herself. "Damn, I forgot, I'm human!"

Kylee climbed back in her bed and thought about her dad and Ja'Nay. The more she thought about her actions, the more fucked up she felt. The last thing she wanted to do was disappoint the two most important people in her life. She lay there trying to think of a way to make it right with them and came up with nothing. Times like this she really hated that I'reon was so far away. She needed someone to talk to so bad; someone to tell her it would be okay. Kylee had grown so dependent on Eli to make her world right; she couldn't wait until he came home from work. Feeling sick to her stomach, Kylee ran to the bathroom and began throwing up. She rinsed her mouth out and walked back into her room. Kylee climbed back in bed, curled up in a ball, and cried.

Chapter Eighteen

It had been a few days short of three weeks since Kylee had last seen her mother. They had talked a few times on the phone, but every time her father walked in the room, her mother would rush her off the phone. Her father was still upset about her moving Eli in and it was putting a serious strain on their relationship. Kylee had a few minutes to spare before her hair appointment so she decided to stop by to visit her mother for a minute, but not before riding by the hotel her father and Sylvia met at every Thursday to make sure they were there. Like clockwork, she saw his car parked in the lot, so she headed over to her parents' house.

"Mom," Kylee called out, using her house key to get in, surprised her father hadn't changed the locks on her.

"I'm in the kitchen," her mother replied while cutting up some fresh vegetables.

"What's up?" Kylee asked, smiling, walking in and giving her mother a kiss on the cheek.

"Hey, baby." Her mother smiled back, happy to see her daughter.

"What you cookin'?" Kylee asked, catching a whiff before walking over to the stove and lifting the top off of one of the pots.

"Spaghetti; why, you want some?" her mother asked, wiping her hand on a dish towel.

"Naw, 'cause 'bout time it gets done, *he'll* be home," Kylee said, taking a seat on the stool.

"*He* who?" her mother turned around and asked.

"You know who *he* is," Kylee replied smartly.

"That *he* is your father, Kylee," her mother stated sternly.

"I can't tell. He sure don't act like it," Kylee said, rolling her eyes.

"Why, because he's upset about you movin' a man up in your house?" her mother asked.

"No, that ain't the reason," Kylee said, knowing it was.

"There can't be any other reason. Ya dad gives you the world," her mother said.

"Gave," Kylee corrected.

"Well, didn't nobody tell you to move a nigga up in ya house knowin' your daddy was payin' the bills. You could still be gettin' the world if you woulda listened to your father," her mother said.

"I'm cool. I don't need him to do nothin' for me. Eli takes good care of me," Kylee bragged.

"Well, I hope you got sense enough to not depend on no nigga. You need to get out and get your own!"

I don't ever remember you goin' out punchin' nobody's time clock, Kylee wanted to say, but out of respect she kept it to herself. "I just don't see the logic behind Daddy's attitude," Kylee said.

"You don't think your father should be upset about you movin' a man in your house after he asked you not to?" her mother questioned.

"No. I can see if Eli was livin' up in there rent free. He pays all the bills. I can see if I moved a broke nigga up in my spot, but I didn't. Eli owns his own businesses and everything," Kylee protested.

"Chile you got a lotta growin' up to do," her mother said, shaking her head before tending to her food.

"You always takin' his side," Kylee huffed.

"I'm not takin' anyone side, Kylee," her mother said, taking the top off the pot and stirring her homemade spaghetti sauce.

"Yes, you are, you always take his side, even when he's wrong," Kylee said, catching an attitude.

"Well, if he doin' it all like that, how come he doesn't have his own house?" her mother questioned.

"He did," Kylee said, leaving it at that.

"Did?" her mother asked.

"Yeah," Kylee huffed, not trying to have her mom all up in Eli's business, giving them something else to throw up in her face.

"Well, what happened to it?" her mother pried.

"I don't know. Look, I'm about to go," Kylee said, standing up from the barstool.

"Already? You just got here. Your father don't come home for lunch on Thursdays so you can stay a little longer, can't you?" her mother asked.

"No, I gotta go get my hair braided."

"Well call me later on, okay?" her mother said, not wanting her daughter to leave.

"I will, Mommy," Kylee said, giving her mother a hug before turning to walk away.

Kylee hopped back in her car and pulled off. Kendrick Lamar's "Swimming Pools" was banging out of the speakers as she pulled up to the red light. She looked over to her left and saw Josh in the car with his wife and instantly got jealous. Kylee could tell he was avoiding turning his head her way on purpose by the way he looked out the corner of his eye.

"No, this bitch ain't frontin' 'cause he wit' his bitch," Kylee said, blowing the horn, catching the attention of his wife. She looked over at Kylee and frowned. Kylee blew Josh a kiss and busted out laughing before speeding off from the light, leaving them in her dust.

Still smiling, Kylee pulled up in front of the African shop and got out. She looked over at the Cadillac she parked next to and instantly recognized it. She pressed the wrinkles out of her clothes, threw her purse strap onto her shoulder, and walked into the shop with her head held high. She walked over to the assortment of hair and picked out the color. The entire time Tionna and Edna were staring her down with mugs on their faces.

"You ready?" asked one of the African braiders as she walked over to Kylee.

"Yep," Kylee answered, following the lady over to an empty chair. The lady sat Kylee across from Tionna and next to Edna. The two friends continued staring at Kylee. Kylee sat down in the chair, looked over at Edna and then at Tionna, and smirked.

"These young hoes really think they be doin' somethin'," Tionna looked over at Edna and said.

"Don't they. You betta than me 'cause I woulda been whooped her ass," Edna said, trying to start some shit.

Kylee didn't respond. They could continue to hold a conversation about her like she wasn't there if they wanted to. As long as they didn't put their hands on her, Kylee was cool with them talking. It was quite entertaining. She didn't want any trouble. All she came there for was to get her hair put in micro braids.

"Whoop her for what? Shit, what she don't understand is me and my husband got a bond that can't be broken," Tionna said with confidence.

Not being able to contain herself, Kylee let out a chuckle.

"You find somethin' funny?" Tionna looked over at Kylee and asked.

"Only the fact that you think Eli is comin' back to you," Kylee replied smartly.

"Look, baby girl, you don't have anything to offer my husband but some ass, so why would he try to build a future with you?" Tionna asked.

Edna and a couple of the other customers snickered.

Embarrassed by the truth because Kylee knew Eli was paying all the bills, plus giving her money to spend, so she really didn't have anything to offer Eli.

"I bet you still livin' at home wit' ya mommy and daddy," Tionna continued.

There was more snickering in the shop.

"Actually, I got my own place, thank you," Kylee replied.

The African lady finished up Tionna's hair and handed her a mirror to look at the finished project. Loving her new look, Tionna handed the lady the mirror back and stood up.

"Look, you might have my husband for now, but mark my words, he'll be back and when he comes home don't say I didn't warn you," Tionna said before turning to walk away, making Kylee feel small in front of the other customers.

"I'll call you when I'm done," Edna called out to Tionna as she headed over to the register to pay for her hairdo.

"Okay," Tionna said, handing the cashier two crisp hundred dollar bills before heading out the door, leaving Kylee feeling small.

Chapter Nineteen

The following day after the incident with Kylee and Tionna at the hair shop, Kylee was in the kitchen cooking dinner when Eli walked in and slammed the door behind him.

"What the fuck?" she asked, wiping her hands on the dish towel before walking out of the kitchen.

"I can't believe this bitch!" Eli said angrily as he walked into the living room.

"What's happened?" Kylee asked.

"I went by the house this mornin' to get some more of my stuff; this bitch done got the locks changed. I'm cool wit' that. But then I go to the daycare when I get off work to see my daughter. And them muthafuckas tell me Tionna took me off Sy'onn's emergency contact form and said not to let me pick her up 'cause I'm gon' kidnap her."

"What?" Kylee frowned.

"Then when I get to flippin' out up in the daycare center, they threatened to call the police on me, so I just dipped! I'ma kill that bitch!" Eli snapped.

"Calm down, baby. We gon' think of somethin'," Kylee said.

"Calm down my ass; this bitch playin' wit' my daughter!" Eli said as he paced back and forth through the living room.

"She knows how you feel about your daughter. That's why she playin' these games wit' you," Kylee explained.

"That bitch know I will do somethin' to her about my daughter! Then when I call the ho, she gon' tell me not to worry about Sy and to have a baby by the bitch pussy I've been eatin'!"

"She too damn old to be actin' like that," Kylee said, shaking her head.

Eli's phone began to ring before he could reply. "Hello?" he answered angrily. "Why the fuck you tell them people I'm gon' kidnap my daughter, T?"

Kylee sat on the sofa and pretended to be occupied with something on TV, but was really listening in on Eli's conversation.

"Bitch, you betta go up there in the mornin' and put my name back on her list or we gon' have some problems. Now think I'm playin' if you want to," he said, hanging up on Tionna before she could respond.

His phone rang right back. He looked at the number on the screen and saw that it was Tionna and didn't bother answering it, tired of arguing. He said what he meant and meant what he said, and Tionna knew him well enough to know that his name better be back on their daughter's list the next morning.

"Other than the bullshit you been goin' through with Tionna, how was your day at work?" Kylee asked.

Eli's phone began ringing again before he could respond. He checked the number and pushed the ignore button. "It was okay. I'm tired though," he said.

"Well go take a shower; dinner will be ready in a few."

"Thanks, baby," he said walking over and giving Kylee a kiss on the lips before heading upstairs. Eli wasn't used to having a hot meal ready for him when he got off work. When he was with Tionna he prepared all the meals. She didn't know the first thing about cooking; only thing she was good at doing was making reservations.

Kylee walked back in the kitchen to finish preparing dinner. She loved the fact that the more Tionna continued doing stupid shit to Eli, the further she was pushing him away. Pretty soon, Eli was going to get fed up and leave Tionna for good and Kylee would be right there for him when he did.

Chapter Twenty

Kylee was lying in the bed dizzy and dripping in sweat. She'd been up all night throwing up. She was thinking she may have gotten food poisoning from the gyros they'd had for dinner. Eli had offered to stay home and take care of her, but she assured him that she would take some Pepto-Bismol and be just fine.

Kylee's cell phone began to ring. She rolled over, picked it up off the nightstand, and forced herself to smile. "Hey, sis," she answered in a groggy tone.

"Ewwww, you sound like you got a man in yo' throat," I'reon joked.

"I feel like I got one in there," she said, laughing.

"You sick or somethin'?"

"Yeah, man, I've been throwin' up all night. I'm dizzy and hot. I think I got food poisonin' from dinner last night."

"Either that or yo' ass pregnant," I'reon said.

"Bitch, please, I am not pregnant," Kylee replied.

"How do you know?" I'reon asked.

"I just do."

"Have you taken a test?"

"No, I don't need to take no test. Eli is very careful when we havin' sex," Kylee said.

"Does he wear condoms?" I'reon questioned.

"Sometimes," Kylee answered.

"Bitch, you pregnant," I'reon repeated.

"No, I'm not, and would you stop sayin' that?" Kylee asked, slightly annoyed.

"If that nigga not wearin' condoms all the time there's a strong chance I'm about to be an auntie," I'reon said, laughing.

"Whatever; what you call me for?" Kylee laughed too, brushing the thought to the side and sticking with food poisoning from the gyro.

"Actually, I was just callin' to check on you and see if things were still goin' well in paradise," I'reon replied.

"Yeah, things are still goin' good between me and Eli, but I ain't gon' lie, sis, in the back of my mind, I still have this fear of him going back to his wife. I would never tell him this, but sometimes I think maybe he should try to work things out wit' Tionna. She is his wife," Kylee said.

"Oh my goodness! Is this really Kylee Ny'Air Hampton I'm talkin' to? Or an imposter?" I'reon joked.

Kylee laughed. "It's me. I just have been thinkin' a lot lately. I can't imagine what she's goin' through. I've never had to experience bein' left before. I'm still not gon' leave him alone even if he does get back wit' her."

"Well, sis, you gotta look at it like this: if he wanted to be wit' Tionna, that's where he would be, but he's not. He's there wit' you. He said himself that he didn't love her, so fuck what she goin' through and focus on you and your happiness."

"You know what, you right; fuck her and what she's goin' through. I don't know what got into me. For a minute I was startin' to act like Ja'Nay," Kylee said, laughing.

"Right," I'reon agreed. "She's rubbin' off on you."

"Please, don't ever let me get that soft. If I do, please slap me back to reality," Kylee joked.

"I got'chu, sis," I'reon said. "Speakin' of Ja'Nay, is she still mad at you?"

"No, she finally got over the initial shock of us startin' school in January instead of August."

"That's good, 'cause she was crushed," I'reon said.

"I know. I felt bad too, but she don't have nothin' to worry about. I got all our paperwork turned in for winter quarter, so all we gotta do is go to school."

"That's wassup! I'm proud of y'all," I'reon said sincerely.

"Thank you."

"All right, sis, I'm about to go. I just wanted to hear your voice. I'm about to call Ja'Nay and check on her, too."

"Okay," Kylee said, not wanting to let her go.

"Oh, I know what else I called you for," I'reon said.

"What?"

"Have you talked to Uncle Vince?"

"Nope," Kylee said. "He's still actin' like a bitch."

"A bitch?" I'reon asked, laughing.

"Yes, a bitch. I don't even care though."

"How you payin' your bills? I mean I'm sure Eli is helpin' out, but you know how you like to shop and shit and since you cut all your boy toys off, how's that workin' out?" I'reon asked.

"My mom still pays my car note and insurance without my dad knowing. Eli pays all the bills and buys the groceries, and as far as me shoppin' like I'm used to, bitch, I still got one boy toy footin' that bill, so I'm cool. You know Mama didn't raise no fool; you know Kylee Ny'Air Hampton has to always keep an ace in the hole."

"I know that's right, sis," I'reon responded happily.

"All right, girl, it feels like I'm about to throw up again," Kylee said, holding her stomach. "I will call you later."

"All right, sis, get you some Vernors. And a pregnancy test," she slid in.

"Whatever." Kylee laughed before hanging up. She lay in the bed a few more seconds, hoping her stomach would settle. Feeling herself about to throw up again, Kylee jumped out of bed and made it to the toilet just in the nick of time.

"God, help me," she called out, feeling like she was about to die. Kylee crawled back into her bedroom, grabbed her cell phone, and called Ja'Nay.

"Hello?" Ja'Nay answered.

"Can you borrow your mom's car and bring me somethin' for my stomach?" she moaned.

"Girl, you sound horrible," Ja'Nay said.

"I feel the same way," Kylee said, wiping beads of sweat away from her forehead.

"I'll be there in about twenty minutes," Ja'Nay said.

"Okay," Kylee said, hanging up and pulling herself back into bed.

Half an hour later, Ja'Nay pulled up with a grocery bag full of things that would hopefully help her best friend feel better. She let herself in with her key and headed straight up to Kylee's room.

"Shit, bitch, it's cold up in here and it smells like throw-up." Ja'Nay grimaced.

"Shut, up, bitch, and I'm burnin' up," Kylee said. "Did you bring the Pepto?"

Ja'Nay sat down on the bed beside her best friend. "Yep, and some Tums, and a ginger ale, and a pregnancy test," she said, pulling each item out the bag.

"Let me guess, you talked to I'reon?" Kylee asked.

"Yep, and she suggested I pick one up for you." Ja'Nay laughed.

"I told that heffa I wasn't pregnant," Kylee said, taking the pregnancy test from Ja'Nay, tossing it on the bed before sitting up.

"Where you 'bouta go?" Ja'Nay asked.

"Uhhhh, I gotta pee; is that okay wit' you?" Kylee asked smartly while scooting out of the bed.

"Here, take this wit'you," Ja'Nay said, picking up the pregnancy test.

"I don't need that, 'cause I'm not pregnant!" Kylee fussed.

"Please just take it. I promised I'reon I would
see to you takin' one," Ja'Nay said.

Kylee sighed. "You two bitches get on my
nerves," she huffed, snatching the test from
Ja'Nay's hand and walking into the bathroom.
Kylee opened the package, placed the stick
underneath her, and peed on the stick. She
then laid the stick on the counter, wiped herself,
washed her hands, and walked back into her
bedroom.

"Well, what did it say? I got I'reon textin' me
tryin'a find out the results," Ja'Nay said.

"I don't know. I peed on the damn thing and
laid it on the sink in the bathroom," she said,
climbing back into bed.

"Ewwww, that's nasty," Ja'Nay laughed.

"It is ain't it?" Kylee laughed, not thinking
about how unsanitary it was when she laid it up
there.

"Well let's go see what the results say," Ja'Nay
said anxiously.

"I can tell you what they say. I'm not pregnant,"
Kylee said.

"Well, just go see," Ja'Nay pushed.

"If you wanna know what it say so bad, you go
check," Kylee said before closing her eyes.

"I sure will." Ja'Nay stood from the bed, walked
in the bathroom, picked up the test, and shook
her head.

"What it say?" Kylee called out from the bed and asked.

"I thought you didn't wanna know," Ja'Nay said smartly.

"For real, for real, I don't 'cause I know I'm not pregnant," Kylee said.

"Well that ain't what this test says," Ja'Nay said, walking in the room with the test in hand.

Kylee's eyes popped open and she sat straight up. "Quit playin', bitch," Kylee said, quickly getting out of bed, snatching the test from Ja'Nay's hand and reading the results for herself. "I'll be damned, I'm pregnant!" Kylee snapped, surprised, starting to feel even sicker.

"What you gon' do?" Ja'Nay asked.

"I don't know," Kylee replied, walking over to her bed and lying down.

"You betta think of somethin'," Ja'Nay said.

"Like what?" Kylee asked, confused.

"Whose is it?" Ja'Nay asked.

Kylee shot her friend a "you already know" look.

"What? Shit, I'm just askin'. You was fuckin' a lotta niggas," Ja'Nay said.

"I been quit fuckin' wit' them niggas, all but Tony. And me and him use protection at all times," Kylee responded.

Kylee and Ja'Nay both sat in silence, trying to come up with a plan.

"Look, I suggest you have an abortion," Ja'Nay finally said.

"Huh?"

"How you gon' go to college and take care of a baby, too? I don't know about you but I'm goin' to school in January. You can sit around here and be mommy to a baby if you want to, that's on you. I'm sorry, I can't rely on my mommy and daddy so I have to make somethin' out of myself," Ja'Nay said harshly.

"I don't know what to do," Kylee said as tears began to fill her eyelids.

"Look, Kylee, your dad already mad at you for not goin' to college in the fall and done cut you off financially. Just think how he's gon' react if you're pregnant and still not gon' be able to go to college? How you gon' take care of a baby? Keep sleepin' wit' Tony?" Ja'Nay asked.

"Eli would help me take care of his child," Kylee said.

"But what if he decides to go back to Tionna? You said yourself you still worried he might try to work things out with her in order to see his daughter," Ja'nay said, hoping to convince Kylee to do the right thing . . . well, the right thing in her eyes.

Even though Kylee hated to admit it, Ja'Nay did make some valid points. She knew her father would disown her if she got pregnant and didn't go to college, but what if Eli really did go back to Tionna? She would be stuck, struggling and taking care of a child when she could barely take care of herself.

"Maybe I should call I'reon and see what she has to say?" Kylee said, second-guessing an abortion.

"No, 'cause she just gon' talk you into havin' it and you the one who's gon' have to take care of it. She lives way over in Spain," Ja'Nay said, trying to keep her from calling I'reon.

"True."

"Look, Kylee, I know right now it doesn't seem like the right thing to do, but you have to think about your future. You'll have plenty of time to have kids."

"I know," Kylee said as the tears flowed.

"Don't cry, we gon' get through this together," Ja'Nay assured her. She took the phone book out of the top drawer of the nightstand and handed it to Kylee.

Kylee wiped her eyes, hoping she was making the right decision as she flipped through the phonebook pages. Stopping on the A's, she dialed the first number she came across.

"Hello?" a woman answered in a pleasant tone.

"Yes, I need to make an appointment."

Chapter Twenty-one

Kylee lay in bed crying and in pain. Ja'Nay had just dropped her off and offered to stay with her until Eli got off work, but Kylee wanted to be alone. She needed time to think about what she'd just done. She couldn't get over the fact that she'd just taken a life and prayed to God that He'd forgive her for doing such a horrible thing.

As Kylee was trying to get some rest, the doorbell rang. She slowly got up and walked to the top of the stairs. "Who is it?" she yelled down asking. No one answered. "I said who is it?"

Getting no answer a second time, Kylee eased down the stairs and looked out the peephole. "What the fuck?" Kylee snatched the door opened. "What the fuck you doin' at my mutha-fuckin' house? Bitch, you done lost your mind, but I'ma whoop yo' ass until you find it," she said to Tionna, knowing she wasn't in any shape to fight anyone, but she sure wasn't about to let Tionna know that.

"Wait, wait, wait, Kylee," Tionna said, holding up her hands trying to stop anything from happening.

"Wait my ass; bitch, you at my house and how the fuck you know my name?"

Tionna looked a hot mess. She looked like she hadn't slept in days. She had big bags underneath her eyes and looked nothing like she had at the gas station or the Dairy Queen that day.

"Have you ever had a man mess around on you?" Tionna asked.

"Hell naw," Kylee snapped.

"Well if you had, you would know that I done my homework until I found out your name, where you live, and what you about," Tionna replied boldly.

"Okay, so what the fuck you want at my house?"

"My husband," Tionna answered desperately.

"Look at you. I know this ain't the same bitch who was at the shop poppin' fly in front of an audience; now you here standin' on my porch, beggin' for your husband back." Kylee smirked.

"Just let me explain, Kylee, please, and after you hear me out, you will never have to worry about me again," Tionna pleaded.

"What you wanna explain? How I do have more than just ass to offer Eli? Oh wait a minute, or how you finally come to realize that Eli is never comin' back to you?" Kylee antagonized her. Kylee's words were cutting into Tionna deep. Kylee was outdone. She couldn't believe how much nerve this chick had to actually walk up on her property and ask for her husband back. The old Kylee would have commenced kicking her ass, but the new, maturing Kylee was going to hear her out first, then kick her ass for coming over to her house.

"Please, just hear me out," Tionna begged.

"You got five minutes, then I'm goin' back to lie down," Kylee said.

Tionna stood quietly, trying to get her thoughts together. She knew this would be her one and only chance to ask Kylee for her husband back.

"Talk," Kylee snapped, tired of waiting.

"Look, Kylee, first I want to apologize for callin' you out of your name at the Dairy Queen," Tionna started. "And for tryin'a front on you at the shop."

"It ain't no biggie," Kylee said.

"Look, I really don't know where to start, but all I can say is I wish you would leave my husband alone. I love Eli, and me and my daughter need him home with us," Tionna said.

"Eli don't love you, and you know he don't." Kylee frowned.

Knowing Kylee knew the truth about Eli's feelings hurt Tionna badly. "He might not love me, but I love him. Truthfully, I didn't at first, but I fell in love with him. And the worst feelin' in the world is seein' the one you love, love someone else," Tionna said as tears filled her eyelids.

Kylee listened as Tionna continued pouring out her heart.

"You just don't know how many nights I sit up and wait for my husband to come home, tell me he's sorry, make love to me, and tell me that he'll never leave me again."

Kylee felt bad and felt her eyes welling up, too. She knew messing around with this woman's husband was bad enough, but taking him from her was even worse and she knew better than anyone that karma was a dangerous bitch!

"It's so hard to wait for somethin' you know might never happen, but it's even harder to give up when you know it's everything you want," Tionna said as the tears poured.

"I'm really sorry, Tionna. I never meant for any of this to happen," Kylee said as tears flowed down her cheeks. "I only planned on sleepin' wit' Eli. I never intended for us to be livin' together or anything."

"It's okay." Tionna was glad that she'd gotten through to Kylee and was even happier that her husband was finally coming home so they could be a family again. Tionna made a promise that when Eli came home she would treat him like the king he was. "I'm so happy you see where I'm comin' from and even happier that you're goin' to leave Eli alone," Tionna said, smiling.

"Who said that?" Kylee asked, surprised.

"I thought you understood where I was comin' from," Tionna said.

"I do understand where you comin' from. But you gotta understand that a lot of people's relationships end badly; if not, they wouldn't have ended in the first place," Kylee said.

"So what are you sayin'?" Tionna asked desperately.

"I'm sayin' why keep chasin' a nigga who's already gone? Focus on your future and not your past," Kylee stated. With that being said, Kylee walked back in the house, leaving Tionna standing on the porch.

Chapter Twenty-two

Kylee was sitting in the living room watching reruns of *Diff'rent Strokes* when Eli walked through the door carrying a dozen red roses.

"Awww, are these for me?" Kylee asked, taking them from his hand.

"Who else would they be for?" he asked, smiling.

"They are so pretty," she replied, before putting them up to her nose to smell them.

"Not as pretty as you," he said, sitting down next to her and kissing her on the cheek before moving his way down to her neck.

"What's the special occasion?" Kylee asked, scooting over.

"You will never guess," he said, still smiling.

"Well just tell me," Kylee said, smiling too.

"Tionna's gon' finally give me a divorce," he said happily.

"How you manage to get her to do that?" Kylee asked, standing up from the sofa.

"She don't have no choice," Eli said, standing up as well.

"What you do?" Kylee inquired impatiently while walking into the kitchen to put the flowers in some water.

"Okay, two weeks ago I had my dude, Chico, from Henry Key & Lock, meet me at my house while Tionna was at work so I could get in the house and get some more of my stuff. Then I had my other dude, Omar, who hooks up security systems, come and put a camera in my bedroom," Eli said while following Kylee into the kitchen.

"What?" Kylee asked, looking around for a camera.

"Ma, I don't have no cameras in here." Eli laughed.

"I don't know," she said playfully.

"Anyways, me, Omar, and Chico went back over there this mornin' and unhooked the cameras, took it back to Omar's shop, and watched the CD. And sure enough she was fuckin' somebody in my bed, just like I suspected a long time ago," Eli said.

"What?" Kylee asked, surprised, knowing the chance of him ever going back to Tionna was over. "Well if you suspected she was cheatin' a long time ago, why you just now decide to put the camera in y'all's room?"

"I was sittin' back waitin' for the right time. There's a right time to do everything. When I met you and fell in love I knew it was the right time."

Kylee's heart fluttered, hearing Eli say he was in love with her for the first time; she felt the same way.

"I never said anything to her about messin' around because she deserved to be happy. I wasn't givin' her what she wanted, so why rain on her parade?"

"Do you know the nigga she was fuckin'?"

"Yep."

"Who?" Kylee pried.

"My nigga, Big Ness," Eli replied, unfazed.

"What the fuck? I thought that was ya boy?" Kylee asked.

"He was; matter of fact, he still is. I ain't mad at him. He could only do what Tionna allowed him to do," Eli said.

"True," Kylee agreed. "So what happened next?"

"I went to her job, popped the DVD in her computer, and when the movie popped on she couldn't say nothin'. I had hours of footage; she was caught in the nude," Eli said, smiling.

"Hell naw." Kylee smiled.

"That's when I started makin' my demands. I told her I wanted a divorce and shared parentin'.

I told her she could have the house, 'cause I bought it for her and Sy'onn. All I want is my clothes, my parents' belongin's, and my two cars and she can have the rest of the shit. I'll start over fresh."

"And she agreed to it just like that?" Kylee asked.

"Just like that. She had no choice. I told her if I showed that tape to my attorney it would tear her ass up in court, even though I wouldn't do no shit like that. That's too much like snitchin' and I hate a snitch! But I'm gettin' what I want." Eli smiled.

"Wow, you crucial."

"Keep that in mind, just in case you try to pull some shady shit." He winked.

"Whatever." Kylee laughed.

"I'm just playin'," Eli said, knowing he was serious as a heart attack.

"I'm happy you finally got what you wanted," Kylee said sincerely.

"I am too. Now all I want to do is celebrate by makin' love to my woman," Eli said, walking over to Kylee and kissing her on her neck.

"Who said I was your woman? We never put a title on our relationship," Kylee said, taking a step back.

"Well, would you be my woman, Kylee Ny'Air Hampton?" Eli asked, smiling.

"I don't know, Eli, a relationship is like a full-time job: you know if you apply for the position, you have to be ready to put in the work," Kylee said.

"I stay ready to work, so gettin' into a relationship wit' you won't be no different," Eli said.

"Promise me, if we gon' do this we gon' do it right wit' no bullshit," Kylee said.

"I promise you, ma. I'm ready to take us to the next level; but if I'm gon' work you gon' work too, okay?"

"Oh, I'm gon' put in my share." Kylee smiled.

"Good, now let me start by workin' on gettin' some of my kitty," Eli said, taking a step closer to Kylee and pulling her into his space.

"We need to eat dinner," Kylee said, trying to stop Eli from getting freaky as he sucked on her neck and fondled her breast. It had only been a little over a week since she'd had the abortion and the doctor told her she had to wait at least two weeks before having sex. Even though she wanted it just as bad as Eli she had to protect herself from getting any type of infection. It had been hard trying to keep Eli away from her. She'd been going to bed fully dressed, pretending to be asleep and even complaining of a headache, but all that was starting to get old. Eli was starting to get suspicious.

"I'd rather eat you," Eli said, as he continued nibbling on her neck while trying to unbutton her shorts.

"Come, on, baby, let's eat before the food gets cold," she said, trying to push him off of her.

"What the fuck is yo' problem? For the last two weeks every time I try to get some pussy, you push me off you, or pretend like you 'sleep!" Eli snapped. "What, you fuckin' somebody else?"

"No," she quickly answered.

"Well, you sure haven't been fuckin' me," he said angrily.

As good as Eli had been to Kylee she knew he deserved the truth, and she was going to give it to him, just not today.

"Look, Eli, I got a yeast infection," Kylee said.

"A what?" Eli asked, frowning.

"A yeast infection," she repeated.

"Where did you get that from? You damn sure didn't get it from me," Eli said defensively.

"All women get yeast infections. You don't get it from anyone."

"Well how come you didn't just tell me instead of avoidin' me?"

"'Cause I was embarrassed," Kylee said.

"When did you find out about this yeast infection?" Eli asked.

"I found out about a week and a half ago when I went to the doctor. She said it came from me wearin' thongs," Kylee lied.

"Well, what you supposed to wear, granny panties?" he joked, easing up on his attitude.

"At least for a couple of months," Kylee said.

"That's not gon' be sexy." Eli smiled.

"Whatever. I can make whatever I put on look sexy," Kylee bragged.

"Well how long it's gon' be before I can get some of that kitty then?"

"At least five more days," she said, wanting it just as bad as Eli.

"Damn, what am I supposed to do until then?" he asked, unzipping his jeans and pulling his Johnson out of the hole in his boxers.

"I can think of one thing," Kylee said, dropping down to her knees and placing Eli's manhood in her wet mouth and pleasing her man, just the way he liked.

Chapter Twenty-three

Eli woke up bright and early, feeling like a new man. His woman was finally able to break him off and he had to admit she'd done an excellent job. Eli fixed Kylee breakfast, put it in the microwave, and decided to detail her car for her just to show his appreciation.

"Hey, Mr. Vernon." Eli smiled and waved as he headed to Kylee's car.

"Hey, Eddie," Mr. Vernon said, waving back.

"Eli," Eli corrected.

"Yeah, Eli," Mr. Vernon replied, forcing a weak smile.

"You a'iiiight?" Eli asked, Mr. Vernon who looked as if he was about to pass out.

"Yeah, I'm good. Just a li'l under the weather that's all. Ain't nothin' a cold Colt 45 can't take care of."

Eli laughed. "Well I'll bring you one back when I'm done detailin' Kylee's car."

"Good lookin'," Mr. Vernon said.

Eli got in Kylee's car and pulled off. He was bumpin' Tupac as he sped down the street. All of a sudden her tire felt and sounded like it was about to fall off. Eli pulled over to the side of the street and got out. He looked down at the almost-flat tire and shook his head. He popped the trunk, grabbed the bag with the jack in it, and opened it up.

"What's this?" he asked himself, pulling a piece of paper out and reading it.

Eli couldn't believe what he was reading. He wanted to kill somebody, preferably Kylee.

"An abortion? Ain't this about a bitch?" He frowned angrily.

Eli couldn't wait to get back to the house; he was going to get to the bottom of this. He put the spare tire on, went to the drive-through, and grabbed Mr. Vernon's beer before heading back to the house.

Eli backed up in the driveway at the house, got out of the car, walked across the yard, and knocked on Mr. Vernon's door. There was no answer. He didn't have time to wait, so he put the beer between the door and the screen door and jogged back across the yard.

"Hey, baby, thanks for the breakfast," Kylee said, smiling, when Eli walked in.

Eli walked in and sat down on the sofa, staring

at Kylee for a brief second. He stood up, and shook his head.

"What the fuck wrong wit' you?" she asked.

"Didn't I ask you not to make me regret this?" Eli asked out of nowhere.

"What are you talkin' about?" Kylee frowned, trying to think back to see if she'd done anything she wasn't supposed to. She knew he hadn't found out about her sneaking over to Tony's whenever she'd gotten the chance, because she made sure she only did that while Eli was at work.

"You know what the fuck I'm talkin' about, Kylee," Eli said, getting angrier by the second.

"Look, I don't know what ya problem is, but you shoulda checked it at *my* front door!" Kylee snapped.

"Fuck you mean, *my,* broad? You don't pay a muthafuckin' thing up in here! Keep talkin'. I'll put yo' ass out," Eli snapped.

"What the fuck is ya problem, Eli?" Kylee asked desperately.

"You wanna know what my problem is? My problem is yo' lyin' ass killed my seed. *If* it was mines and, yeah, I said *if*," Eli said, mean mugging Kylee.

Kylee's mouth hit the floor. How in the world did he find out about her getting an abortion?

The only people who knew other than her and Ja'Nay were the people at the clinic.

"Close ya mouth," Eli said smartly. "I can't believe you would do some foul shit like that!"

Kylee had completely forgotten about hiding that paperwork in her trunk. Her intentions were to throw the paper away as soon as she got the chance, but she'd forgotten.

"What the fuck was you doin' goin' through my trunk?" was all she could come up with.

"Bitch, I was changin' ya tire if you really must know!" Eli snapped.

"Bitch?" Kylee asked.

"Yeah, bitch," Eli repeated.

"Look, you ain't gon' talk to me like you be talkin' to that old ho!"

"You right, I'm not. I'm gon' talk to you like a young ho," Eli said, pointing his finger in Kylee's face, trying to refrain from putting his paws on her.

Kylee was actually scared. She'd never seen Eli this mad before. She wasn't sure what he might do to her so she decided to leave until he calmed down. She got up from the sofa, grabbed her keys off the ottoman, and headed toward the door.

"Where the fuck you 'bouta go? I ain't done talkin'." Eli grimaced.

"I'm 'bouta go to my parents' house until you calm down," Kylee said nervously as her heart raced.

"What you leavin' for? I ain't gon' do nothin' to you, I don't hit women," Eli assured her.

Kylee still wasn't comfortable with staying, just in case Eli decided to snap.

"I'm just gon' go," Kylee said, walking toward the door, hoping he would let her leave without any problems.

"Yeah, get the fuck outta my face before I spit on you," he threatened. Eli would never do anything to physically hurt a woman but he would definitely spit on one.

Kylee didn't respond; she just hurried out to her car, got in, and pulled off as fast as she could.

After Kylee had left, Eli couldn't take it. He was sitting around thinking about the death of his parents, not being in his only child's life full time, and, on top of all that, his girl killing his unborn child. This was too much. He walked in the kitchen, grabbed Kylee's fifth of Belvedere and began taking it to the head.

By nine o'clock that night, Eli was sloppy drunk. He was sitting on the sofa watching *The Hangover* when there was a knock on the door.

He looked over at the clock and attempted to get up off the sofa. After the third try he succeeded.

"'Bout time this bitch came home," he said as he stumbled to the door with the bottle still in his hand. Eli swung the door open and was surprised to see Ja'Nay standing there.

"Is Kylee here?" Ja'Nay asked.

"Naw," Eli answered.

"Are you okay?" Ja'Nay asked, eyeing the half-empty bottle while stepping in.

"Yeah, I'm a'iiiight. Are you?" he asked smartly.

"Do you know where Kylee is?" Ja'Nay asked, looking around.

"Hell I don't know. Look, I need to sit down; the room is spinnin'," Eli said, putting the bottle back up to his lips and taking a swig.

"Come on, Eli, let me help you to the sofa," Ja'Nay said, grabbing Eli by the arm as he swayed back and forth.

"Get off of me! I don't need no help," he slurred.

"Is everything okay over here?" Ja'Nay asked, concerned.

"Yeah, why wouldn't it be? Naw, it ain't, I ain't even gon' lie. I can't believe Kylee killed my baby," Eli said, breaking down from the combination of hurt feelings and liquor.

"Come on, Eli," Ja'Nay said, grabbing his arm again, leading him over to the sofa. This time

Eli didn't resist. Ja'Nay helped Eli sit down. She took the bottle from his hand and set it on the floor next to the sofa. "You gon' be okay until Kylee gets home?" Ja'Nay asked.

Eli shook his head yes.

"Okay, well tell her to call me. I'm goin' to spend the night wit' Quann before he turns himself in tomorrow," Ja'Nay said, standing up.

"Wait, don't leave," Eli said, grabbing Ja'Nay by the arm. "Just wait a few minutes. Kylee will be back soon."

Ja'Nay looked at the clock. She had at least an hour before she was supposed to meet Quann, so babysitting Eli for a little while wouldn't hurt.

"What you see in Quann?" Eli looked over and asked Ja'Nay, seeing two of her.

"I don't know. He's nice when he wanna be," Ja'Nay answered.

"Kylee said he be doggin' you. Why you fuck wit' a nigga who don't respect you?" Eli asked.

Ja'Nay was feeling some type of way about Kylee telling Eli her business. "He don't be doggin' me," Ja'Nay lied.

"Fuckin' any- and everybody ain't doggin' you?" Eli asked.

"What?" Ja'Nay frowned.

"Look, don't tell Kylee I told you that. I wasn't supposed to say shit," Eli said.

"I won't," Ja'Nay said. She couldn't wait to cuss Kylee out for telling Eli her business.

Eli stared at Ja'Nay for a brief second. "You a pretty girl; stop lettin' niggas dog you, okay?" Eli said as if he were scolding her.

"I will," she said, checking Eli out.

"You promise?" Eli asked.

"I promise." Ja'Nay smiled.

"You look nice in ya little mini skirt," Eli said, reaching over tugging at Ja'Nay's skirt.

"Thank you," Ja'Nay said.

Eli kept stopping in midsentence and staring over at Ja'Nay.

"You know Kylee had an abortion?" he asked, hurt.

"Yeah, I know," Ja'Nay answered, considering it payback for her telling him all her business.

"Wow, that's fucked up. She killed my seed," Eli said, shaking his head. "Then gon' try to tell me we couldn't fuck 'cause she had a yeast infection. Naw, we couldn't fuck 'cause you had a muthafuckin' abortion!" The thought made Eli angry all over again.

Ja'Nay didn't respond.

"Would you ever kill Quann's child?"

"Naw, I don't believe in abortions," Ja'Nay answered.

"That's what I'm talkin' about," Eli said, laying his hand on Ja'Nay's leg.

Ja'Nay knew Eli was drunk and out of line for touching her, but she didn't make him move his hand.

"I don't know why Kylee killed my baby. That's real fucked up. She knows I lost both parents, I barely get to see my only child; then she just gon' take this chance away from me and I don't know why," he said, breaking down again.

"Don't cry," Ja'Nay said, reaching over and comforting Eli with a hug. Eli laid his head on Ja'Nay's shoulder and cried.

"I'm sorry," he said, lifting his head up while staring in Ja'Nay's eyes.

"It's okay," Ja'Nay said. Eli was close enough to Ja'Nay's face for her to smell the liquor coming off his breath.

"Look at me, I'm a mess," Eli said, wiping his hands down his face as if that was going to sober him up.

"You good," Ja'Nay said.

"Are you sure?"

Ja'Nay shook her head yes, and before she saw it coming, Eli had leaned in and begun kissing her lips. She knew she was dead wrong and should have pushed him off of her, but something inside of her just wouldn't let her.

Eli's hand ventured up her leg and into her panty-less crotch. Ja'Nay threw her head back as Eli finger fucked her using two fingers.

"Ummmm," she moaned as she pushed up against Eli's fingers.

Eli quickly unzipped his pants and pulled his Johnson out. Ja'Nay sized it up and instantly understood why Kylee was so crazy about this nigga. She pulled her skirt up, threw her leg over his, and slid her dripping wet cave down on his dick and began riding him. She wanted to feel what Kylee was always bragging about. Something must have snapped in Eli's head, because without warning, he shoved Ja'Nay off of him and jumped up.

"Get the fuck out!" he yelled, as if what just happened between them was all Ja'Nay's fault.

Ja'Nay pulled her skirt down without opening her mouth. She couldn't believe what she'd just done. She couldn't even look at Eli. Part of her felt horrible at betraying her best friend, but another part of her felt justified for all the shit Kylee was always talking. True enough Kylee didn't know her and Eli had just fucked, but Ja'Nay knowing gave her a weird sense of satisfaction. She was torn as she hung her head and walked out the door, wondering if Eli was going to tell Kylee.

Chapter Twenty-four

It was after two in the morning when Kylee returned home. She'd been driving around all day, waiting, and hoping Eli had calmed down. After sitting in the park for several hours, going to the mall to do a little shopping, and taking herself to a movie, Kylee decided to come home. She lay her keys down on the table in the foyer before walking in the living room. She looked down at Eli, who was passed out on the sofa, snoring loudly. She picked up the half-empty bottle of Belvedere that sat in front of the sofa and took it in the kitchen. She walked back in the living room, leaned down, and kissed Eli on the forehead before heading up to bed.

Eli woke up the next morning with a pounding headache. He looked around the living room like he was in a foreign place. He slowly got up off the sofa and grabbed his head as the room began spinning.

"Kylee," he called out as he began feeling sick to his stomach. Eli stumbled his way upstairs. He busted in the room, scaring Kylee half to death as he ran to the bathroom, missing the toilet, and throwing up all over the floor.

Kylee jumped out of the bed to go check on Eli. "You okay?" she asked, pulling his locks out of the way as he continued throwing up, sounding like it was coming from deep down.

"Oh my God," Eli called out as he continued vomiting. He threw up until there was nothing left in his stomach.

"A drunk ain't shit," Kylee said, grabbing a towel out of the linen closet, running it under some cold water, and wiping Eli's face and mouth.

"Oh, my God," Eli chanted over and over.

Kylee walked downstairs, grabbed the Tylenol, shook three in her hand, and poured a glass of Vernors and took it up to Eli.

"Here," she said, sticking the pills in his mouth and feeding him the pop.

"Help me," he begged.

"Come on," Kylee said, helping Eli up off the floor and walking him over to the bed. Kylee removed Eli's shoes, closed the blinds, and lay in the bed beside him.

"I love you, Kylee," he mumbled.

"I love you too," Kylee said, kissing Eli on the lips before they both drifted back off to sleep.

Two hours later, Kylee woke up to the sound of loud talking outside. It sounded more like screams. Kylee got up to see what was going on. She walked over to her bedroom window and looked down at the crowd of people standing in Mr. Vernon's yard along with the police, fire truck, and ambulance.

"What the fuck? Eli, get up," Kylee shouted frantically.

"What's the matter?" he asked, jumping up.

"Somethin' is goin' on over at Mr. Vernon's. The ambulance is over there," she said, scared.

Eli jumped out of bed, walked over to the window, and needed to know what was going on. He rushed down the stairs to find out what was going on with Kylee close behind. They both walked out on the porch. They noticed a lady screaming out, "Daddy," while an officer tried to calm her down. Kylee was confused, trying to figure out what was going on.

Eli and Kylee both walked over in Mr. Vernon's yard as the neighbors gathered around.

"What happened?" Eli asked the old white guy from across the street.

"Mr. Vernon's daughter came over to check on her father after he wouldn't answer the phone. When she went in, she found him sitting in his chair, dead. He apparently had a heart attack," he said.

"Oh my God, no," Kylee screamed, breaking down. Eli grabbed hold of Kylee as she cried uncontrollably. She began feeling bad all over again about how she'd spoken to him that one day, when all he was trying to do was be nice to her.

Eli couldn't help himself. He wasn't trying to cry in front of Kylee, he didn't want to seem like less of a man, but he couldn't help it, tears steadily flowed as Kylee cried in his arms. He watched as the paramedics wheeled Mr. Vernon's body out of the house on a gurney. Eli looked up on the porch at the can of Colt 45 he had bought Mr. Vernon the day before. Eli couldn't help but think that Mr. Vernon had passed shortly after he'd left, because the beer was still unopened.

After all the commotion died down, Kylee went back into the house and got back in bed. Tears flowed steadily as she lay in bed. She couldn't believe Mr. Vernon was actually gone. Eli had done everything he could to comfort Kylee but it was no use.

"I made you some tea," Eli said, walking upstairs with a mug in hand.

Kylee didn't respond. She just lay in bed with a blank stare.

"I'ma set it down on the nightstand and whenever you feel like drinkin' it, it'll be here," he said.

Kylee still didn't respond. Eli set the mug down and headed back downstairs. Kylee's phone began to ring. She looked at the number and answered it, needing to hear a comforting voice.

"Hello?" she answered.

"You okay?" Ja'Nay asked, sensing Kylee had been crying.

"No," Kylee said, as the tears began flowing steadily.

"What's the matter?" she asked, hoping Eli didn't break down and tell her what had gone down between them.

"Mr. Vernon passed away," Kylee cried.

"Awww, did he?" she asked, relieved that was all it was.

"Yeah, man. I can't believe it," Kylee said, wiping her tears away only to have more follow.

"Where's Eli?" Ja'Nay asked.

"He's here, why?" Kylee asked, thinking nothing of it.

"Oh, nothin'. I just wanted to make sure you weren't home alone while you're grievin,' that's all," Ja'Nay lied.

"Oh, okay. Where you at?" Kylee asked.

"I'm at home now. I spent the night wit' Quann last night. You know he had to turn himself in this mornin'," Ja'Nay said.

"Oh, yeah, that's right. What y'all do last night?"

"Fucked, fucked some more, and fucked some more," Ja'Nay said, laughing.

"Ewwwww, you coulda kept that to yourself," Kylee said, laughing, glad her friend was able to put a smile on her face.

"You hungry?" Eli walked in the room and asked. "Oh you on the phone, my bad."

"Oh, I'm just talkin' to Ja'Nay," Kylee said.

The mention of Ja'Nay's name brought back all the memories from the night before.

Oh, shit, Eli thought, hoping Ja'Nay wasn't telling Kylee what went down between the two of them. Eli walked over to the closet, pretending like he was looking for something so he could listen to Kylee's conversation.

"Okay, girl, I'm glad you enjoyed yourself last night. I'm about to get up, I've been in this bed all day," Kylee said.

That bitch told, Eli thought as he pulled out his duffle bag, getting ready to pack his clothes again.

"Okay, talk to you later," Ja'Nay said, hanging up.

"What you doin' with that bag?" Kylee asked, getting out of bed.

"Nothin', I was lookin' for my Nike T-shirt," he said, relieved.

"Oh, check in the dryer. Remember you wore it to the gym," Kylee said, walking past Eli to go into the bathroom to get in the shower.

"Oh, yeah," Eli said, feeling foolish for over-reacting. Eli should have known Ja'Nay wasn't going to tell Kylee because if she did, Kylee could only whoop one ass and that would be hers.

Kylee got dressed and decided to get out of the house. With the passing of Mr. Vernon and her god-sister moving back to Spain, she was in need of some serious therapy, so she called Ja'Nay back to see if she wanted to go shopping.

"Where you 'bouta go?" Eli looked away from the basketball game and asked Kylee when she came down the stairs.

"To the mall wit' Ja'Nay," she replied, grabbing her purse and keys.

Hearing Ja'Nay's name made Eli cringe. He had hoped that she wouldn't start feeling bad and break down and tell Kylee what happened between them. That was a secret he would take to the grave with him.

"How come you didn't ask me if I wanted to go to the mall wit' you?" he stood up and asked, not wanting her to be around Ja'Nay alone.

"What? Kylee asked, confused. "Any other time I ask you to go shoppin' wit' me you just hand me money and tell me to call Ja'Nay or somethin'. You say I stay in the stores too long for you."

"You do, but I just wanna spend some time wit' you," Eli said, grabbing her by the waist and pulling her in to his body.

"Damn, baby, I spend all my time wit' you. It's been a minute since I hung out wit' Ja'Nay; we need to play catch up on girl talk, or gossip as you call it," Kylee said, smiling.

"We can gossip," Eli said, trying his hardest to get Kylee to stay at home.

"Eli, you hate it when I gossip, so I know you ain't about to sit here and share shit wit' me." Kylee laughed.

"Yes, I will, come over here and sit down." Eli grabbed Kylee by the hand and lead her over to the sofa. "What you wanna know?" he asked, sitting down.

Kylee took a seat next to Eli and began asking her questions. "Who all Big Ness messin' around wit'?" she started.

Eli looked at Kylee. He should have known she would ask questions that he couldn't go against the *code* and answer.

"Ask me somethin' else," Eli said, refusing to answer that particular question.

"Come on, Eli, you ain't right!" Kylee whined. "I wanna know the answer to the question I just asked. I know it's some of everybody, just put some names to it."

"Naw, baby, ask me somethin' else. I can't go around tellin' my nigga's business like that. He's like a brother to me," Eli said, shaking his head no.

"What type of gossiper you know pick and choose what they will and will not tell you? Call me when you learn how to gossip," Kylee said, standing up from the sofa. "I'm about to go get Ja'Nay; now she knows how to gossip."

"Well, why you wanna know who Big Ness messin' around wit' in the first place?" Eli wondered.

"I was just bein' nosey. That's why it's called gossipin', somethin' you don't know nothin' about. So I will see you when I get back from the mall with Ja'Nay." Kylee leaned down, kissed Eli on his forehead, and headed for the door.

"Shit," Eli sat back and said and tried to continue to watch the game.

Twenty minutes later, Kylee pulled up in front of Ja'Nay's and blew the horn. Ja'Nay ran out of the house and got in the car. They laughed, talked, and gossiped on their way to the mall.

"What we come to the mall to get?" Ja'Nay asked as they walked into Abercrombie & Fitch.

"I need to pick up some skinny sweatpants. It's startin' to get cold out," Kylee answered while pulling three different colors off the rack before grabbing the fleece hoodies to match.

"It is gettin' cold out," Ja'Nay said, picking out a pair for herself.

"For real, for real, I just wanted to get outta the house. I love Eli and all, but I needed to get away. I was startin' to feel closed in."

"Closed in?"

"Yeah, 'cause I spend all my time wit' Eli. From the time he gets off work we are together and I'm not used to that. I'm used to bein' at home by myself."

"I feel you, but shit I wish I had somebody to share my house wit'," Ja'Nay said wishfully.

"You do, your mom." Kylee laughed.

Ja'Nay laughed too.

"Naw, but for real, sometimes it's cool and then other times I be wishin' he wasn't there. I know it sounds crazy, but it's true. I'm just glad I have you to keep me sane at times like this," Kylee said sincerely.

Ja'Nay had already been feeling remorseful about what had gone down between her and Eli. The more Kylee spoke about their friendship and how much it meant to her, the more Ja'Nay wanted to come clean, but she knew that would be one of the biggest mistakes she could ever make. "You ready?" Ja'Nay asked, feeling uncomfortable.

"Dang, that's all you gettin'?" Kylee asked, noticing Ja'Nay only had one item in her hand.

"Yeah, I'm really not in the mood to do much shoppin' today."

"Well, why did you agree to come?" Kylee asked.

"'Cause you asked me to," Ja'Nay replied.

"See, that's why you my muthafucka!" Kylee smiled.

"And you're mines too." Ja'Nay smiled back as the guilt ate away at her.

Kylee and Ja'Nay continued shopping for the next two hours, before stopping to grab themselves something to eat. Kylee then dropped Ja'Nay off at home before going home to sit right back up under Eli.

Chapter Twenty-five

As the fall months turned into winter, Ja'Nay tried her best to hide her pregnancy. Baggy clothes became a huge part of her wardrobe; even her own mother hadn't noticed her daughter was pregnant. Ja'Nay kept it from everybody including Kylee and Quann. Fearing Quann might try to make her get rid of it so she decided to break the news to him when she was too far along to have an abortion. She knew keeping it from Kylee was wrong, but she'd definitely try to talk her into getting an abortion, not only because Ja'nay had talked her into getting one, but because it was Quann's baby and she knew how Kylee felt about him. Ja'Nay knew what was best for her and having Quann's firstborn would be the only way to keep him and just maybe he would start treating her like Eli treated Kylee.

Ja'Nay lay around the house all day waitin' for Quann to call. She loved talking to him. It seemed like since he'd been locked up, he'd been acting like he needed her more, which had her feeling like finally she would not only be his number one, but his only one. And with the baby coming, she was sure he would love her even more. Ja'Nay started smiling when she saw the institution phone number pop up on her screen.

"Hello?" she answered, smiling.

"You have a collect call from Quann," the recording said.

Ja'Nay waited for the recording to prompt her to press zero to accept the call.

"Hello?" Quann said.

"Hey, baby," she answered.

"What you been doin' all day?" Quann asked.

"Nothin' really. I just got back from the doctor not too long ago," Ja'Nay said.

"What's wrong wit'you?"

"Pregnant," Ja'Nay said, and waited for Quann to start congratulting her and telling her how happy he was and how he couldn't wait to come home to her and his baby.

"By who?" Quann asked instead.

"By you, nigga, who else?" Ja'Nay snapped, offended that he had the nerve to even question her loyalty toward him.

"Shiiiit, you ain't pregnant by me." Quann frowned.

"Who else am I'm pregnant by, nigga? You the only one I been wit'," Ja'Nay argued.

"Check dig, bitch, I can't have no kids. If I could don't you think I would have about a hundred of them li'l muthafuckas runnin' around?" Quann asked.

"Quann, quit playin'," Ja'Nay replied, knowing what Quann had just said was true. As long as she'd been messing around with him, she had never heard him mention having any children.

"Look, I'm not playin'. When I got in that bike accident and had to have surgery when I was a little boy, the doctor told my mom that I would never be able to have kids."

"Yeah, right," Ja'Nay said, starting to get nervous.

"Call my mom and ask her."

"I am," Ja'Nay said, hoping Quann was just really lying to her, like he'd always done.

"In the meantime, bitch, you need to find ya baby daddy, I'm out!" Quann said, hanging up the phone.

"I can't stand this lyin', bitch-ass nigga," Ja'Nay said, quickly dialing Quann's mom's number and waiting for her to answer.

"Hello?" she answered.

"Hi, Ms. Diane?"

"Yes."

"How you been?" Ja'Nay asked.

"I've been good. Who is this, Monique?" Quann's mom asked.

"No."

"Rachel?"

"No," Ja'Nay replied, irritated.

"Trenity?"

"No, it's Ja'Nay," she huffed.

"Well shit, Quann got so many broads I couldn't catch the voice," his mother replied while puffing on a cigarette.

Ja'Nay rolled her eyes. "I got somethin' to ask you," Ja'Nay said.

"I hope you ain't about to ask me for no money for no abortion 'cause you pregnant by my son. If you are you tellin' a damn lie, 'cause Quann can't have any kids," his mother snapped, answering Ja'Nay's question. "Now what is it?"

"Never mind," Ja'Nay said, hanging up the phone.

Ja'Nay was in a state of panic; if it wasn't Quann's, the only other person she'd been with was Eli. How in the world did she get herself in this mess? Trying to be slick and run game on Quann backfired. If only she would have told him earlier about the baby, she would have known he couldn't have kids in time; now she was stuck having a baby by her best friend's man.

Ja'Nay knew she couldn't tell Kylee she was pregnant by Eli; she would have no understanding. Feeling lonely and afraid, Ja'Nay was at a loss. She didn't know what to do so she decided to do what she thought was best: she called to Sy'onn's to see if Eli was there. When they called him to the phone, Ja'Nay hung up and headed down there. She knew she couldn't tell him this devastating news over the phone; she had to tell him face to face.

Ja'Nay walked into Sy'onn's and nervously looked around. She didn't know what to expect. She knew Eli wasn't going to take the news well, and she wasn't expecting him to.

Eli came from behind the black curtain when he saw Ja'Nay on the security camera. "What you want?" he asked, frowning.

This had been the first time they'd been around each other since that night; they had definitely been avoiding one another.

Ja'Nay's heart beat fast. She didn't know how to tell Eli she was pregnant by him and she knew if she waited any longer, she wouldn't go through with it, so she just blurted it out.

"I'm pregnant," she said.

"And? What the fuck you tellin' me for?" He grimaced.

Ja'Nay took a deep breath before speaking. "It's yours," she said, bracing herself for what was about to come out of Eli's mouth.

"You a muthafuckin' liar. It ain't none of mines. I fucked you for all of what, two minutes?" he asked loudly.

"Look, Quann can't have kids and the only other person I been wit' was you," Ja'Nay explained.

Eli rubbed his hand down his face. "Tell me you just playin'?" Eli asked, not wanting to believe this.

"I wish I was playin'," Ja'Nay said as tears formed in her eyes and began streaming down her cheeks.

Seeing the tears, Eli had no choice but to almost believe Ja'Nay. "Shit!" Eli shook his head, wishing he could go back to that night he'd gotten drunk and take everything back. "Well you gon' have to have an abortion," Eli demanded. "I ain't about to lose Kylee over no bullshit that never was meant to happen!"

"I can't," Ja'Nay said, wiping the tears away.

"Why not?"

"I'm too far along."

"Man, this is some bullshit," Eli said, disgusted.

"Kylee gon' kill me," Ja'Nay cried.

"How am I gon' tell the woman I love that I got a baby on the way by her best friend?" Eli asked himself out loud.

"I don't know," Ja'Nay answered, even though Eli wasn't asking her.

Eli looked at Ja'Nay and wanted to slap her for allowing him to fuck her. "Look, are you sure it's mines?"

"Yes, I'm sure," Ja'Nay answered.

"Damn!" he said, shaking his head. "Look, let me tell Kylee myself, 'cause if you tell her, she gon' beat yo' ass, pregnant or not." Ja'Nay knew Eli was telling the truth. "I don't know what the outcome gon' be, but whateva it is I'm gon' have to live wit' it. I'ma tell you this: if this is my baby, I will take care of it, but you, I want you to stay the fuck outta my lane," Eli said, turning to walk away.

Chapter Twenty-six

For the next two weeks Eli tried to come up with ways to break the news to Kylee about the baby, but every time he came close, his nerves got in the way. He tried his best to avoid her, by coming home from work, showering, and going straight to bed. He knew eventually he would have to break down and tell her. He prayed he didn't lose her over one stupid mistake.

For the past two weeks Kylee had noticed a huge change in Eli. She didn't know what wrong with him. He would come home from work, take a shower, and go straight to bed as if he was trying to avoid her. She would catch him zoning in and out at times. She did everything she could do to cheer him up. He would be happy for the moment, then he would go right back to the way he was. Kylee started thinking maybe he was regretting leaving Tionna for her and wanted to go back home but just didn't know how to tell her. Whatever was bothering Eli, Kylee prayed he would just talk to her so they could get through it together and move on with their lives.

"Girl, I don't know what Eli's problem is," Kylee said as she talked to I'reon about Eli's behavior.

"Maybe he's missin' his parents, who knows. You know niggas say we moody, but they the ones who be actin' like they be on they periods," I'reon said, laughing.

"Or maybe he's missin' Tionna," Kylee said.

"Girl, please, that nigga love you. He got to; you killed his child and he forgave you. He left his wife for you. So, girl, if that ain't love I don't know what is," I'reon said, making Kylee think that Eli really did love her.

"That's true. I guess he does love me," Kylee said, smiling.

"Girl, you his boo thang." I'reon laughed.

"He really does make me happy. I just want him to know that whatever's on his mind I'm open to talk about it."

"Well you gon' have to tell him that then," I'reon suggested.

"I am, as soon as he gets off work."

"You heard from Ja'Nay?" I'reon asked.

"Nope, I haven't talked to Ja'Nay in about two weeks. Every time I call her it goes straight to voicemail," Kylee answered.

"I tried callin' her a couple of times too, but she didn't answer for me either. You think she's okay?"

"Hell yeah, she's a'iiiight; that bitch over there sucka strokin' over Quann," Kylee said laughing.

"Damn, she actin' like they gave the nigga twenty years. Shit he'll be out in about fifteen months. That bitch betta get over it!" I'reon said, smacking her lips.

"I'm hip. Shit, 'cause if her ass was the one locked up, that nigga wouldn't be sittin' around all depressed over her ass," Kylee said.

"He sure wouldn't be, but oh well, it's her life," I'reon said, washing her hands of the situation.

"True, it is. Hopefully one day she wakes up and see that nigga ain't gon' change and he damn sure ain't gon' ever be shit," Kylee said.

"So are you excited about goin' to school next month?" I'reon asked, changing the subject to something more positive.

"Girl, yes! I can't wait to get outta here," Kylee said, excited.

"So what Eli gon' do while you're in school?"

"He's gon' get his businesses situated around here then eventually he'll be movin' out to Cali wit' me and start a business of some sort," Kylee replied.

"That's wassup! I'm glad he's supportive of your decision and is willin' to follow his woman while you fulfill your dreams! Damn you got a good one!" I'reon said, happy for her girl.

"Yeah, God blessed me wit' a good one this time and I'm gon' do everything in my power to hold on to him, no matter what," Kylee said sincerely.

"You betta, sis," I'reon warned.

"I am, I promise."

"Okay."

"All right, let me get off here. I hear Eli's keys jingling," Kylee said.

"All right, I love you, sis."

"Love you too," Kylee said, before hanging up. Kylee sat on the sofa and picked up a magazine, acting like she was reading it.

"Hey, baby," Kylee looked at Eli and spoke when he walked into the living room.

"Sup, baby," he replied, walking over and giving her a kiss on the lips before taking a seat on the sofa next to her.

Kylee noticed the blank stare on Eli's face. His actions were starting to take somewhat of a toll on her. She needed to get to the bottom of what was going on in his life.

"Look, Eli, I know somethin' has been botherin' you for a couple of weeks," Kylee started. "I don't know what it is, but I do want you to know that I'm here for you if you need to talk."

Eli looked over at Kylee with a glassy look in his eyes. If she didn't know any better, she would have sworn they were tears.

"And I don't like thinkin' like this, but I hope you're not really regrettin' leavin' Tionna for me," she continued, just needing to know if that's what was bothering him.

Eli shook his head no. "Neva' that! Tionna is the last thing on my mind. I knew the first time I spent the night wit' you I made the right choice by leavin' her. I love you, Kylee."

Kylee had a lump form in her throat. "It means so much to me to even know that I'm loved by you. You have been the missin' link in my chain and now that I have you, my life is complete and I will let nothin' and no one come in between that," Kylee said, meaning every word.

"That's wassup!" Eli smiled; hearing that nothing could tear them apart gave Eli confidence to go ahead and tell her about the baby.

Kylee leaned over and gave Eli a kiss. "I'm about to go finish dinner," she said, standing up, and began walking away.

"Kylee, I do need to talk," Eli called out.

Kylee stopped and turned back around, glad Eli was finally ready to release whatever he'd had bottle up inside of him.

Eli had butterflies in his stomach.

"Okay, baby." She smiled, walking back over and taking a seat next to him on the sofa. "Wassup?"

"Kylee, remember you said you would let nothin' come between us?" Eli asked.

Kylee slowly shook her head yes.

"Did you really mean that?"

"Yeah, I meant it," she said, wondering where this conversation was heading.

Eli took a deep breath before speaking. "I might have a baby on the way," he blurted out.

Kylee was at a loss. She sat and stared at Eli like he was a complete stranger as the news marinated. Without thought, Kylee hauled off and punched Eli in the face. He and Kylee both jumped up off the sofa at the same time.

"What the fuck is wrong wit' you! You done lost yo' fuckin' mind?" Eli asked angrily. He expected Kylee to be upset, but to put her hands on him was something he never expected. Kylee's punch didn't hurt; he was more shocked that she'd had enough nerve to hit him. He'd never been hit in the face before.

"Who you been fuckin', Eli?" Kylee snapped. "Let me guess, Tionna?"

"No," he quickly answered.

"I shoulda known yo' bitch ass wasn't shit from the giddy-up," Kylee screamed.

"Baby, I'm sorry," Eli pleaded.

"I can't believe this shit," Kylee said as tears rushed down her cheeks, ignoring Eli. Eli attempted to wipe her tears away, but she knocked his hand away. "Don't fuckin' touch me, nigga!" she hollered.

"Can you calm down so we can talk?" Eli asked.

"Who is she?" Kylee asked, wiping her own tears away, only to have more follow. "She had to have meant somethin' to you 'cause you fucked the bitch without protection, wow, and now yo' ass got a baby on the way." Kylee shook her head while waiting for him to tell her that he was just playing.

"I said I might have one on the way and the bitch meant nothin' to me. I only fucked her once," Eli said, hoping it would make the situation better, but it didn't.

"Who is she?" Kylee asked, needing to know.

"Promise me you won't get mad," he said.

"You gotta' be fuckin' kiddin' me. Promise you I won't get mad? Nigga, I wouldn't give a fuck if you got Michelle Obama pregnant, nigga, I'm still gon' be mad regardless!"Kylee snapped. "Nigga, you got a muthafuckin' baby on the way!"

"Might," Eli corrected.

"Might my ass! Who the fuck is she?" Kylee said in a demanding tone.

"Ja'Nay," he quickly answered, tired of holding it in.

"Ja'Nay who?" Kylee snapped.

Eli didn't answer.

"I know you ain't talkin' about my so-called best friend?" Kylee asked, hoping Eli knew another Ja'Nay.

Eli slowly shook his head yes.

Kylee instantly snapped. She charged Eli like a raging bull, swinging wildly. She knew she couldn't whoop him, but she sure was going to try. Eli blocked all of Kylee's hits. He'd never had a woman go off on him the way she was. He grabbed her arms and pinned them down to her side.

"Get the fuck off me, Eli," she screamed as she tried to get loose.

"I will when you calm yo' ass down!"

"Please get off me," she begged.

"If you let me tell you how it went down between me and Ja'Nay," he said.

She vehemently shook her head no. "I don't wanna know. I don't care, y'all foul," she cried as she continued to struggle to get loose; but there was no use, Eli was too strong.

"You do care, Kylee. Just let me explain. Will you at least allow me to do that?" he asked.

Kylee knew the only way Eli was going to let her go was if she listened to what he had to say, so she agreed to at least hear him out. "Talk," she said out of breath.

Eli told Kylee how things led up to him sleeping with Ja'Nay after their argument about the abortion, all that he could remember. He told her that it was no longer than three or four minutes before he realized what was happening and made her leave. The more Kylee listened the angrier she got. How could the two people she trusted most betray her like they did?

"I swear to you, Kylee, I never meant for this shit to happen," Eli said truthfully. It hurt Eli to his heart to see Kylee cry over him. Even though his words sounded sincere, she still wanted to spit in his face, but she knew better. He'd already let her get away with hitting him and calling him out his name, which were two things he had asked her to never do. "I refuse to let you go. I know you might be upset right now, and you have the right to be, but like you said, we can't let nothin' and no one come between what we built together."

Kylee was hurt and outdone by what Eli had just revealed to her. She knew she still loved him, but didn't know how to really react to what he'd just said to her. Sleeping with her best friend was crossing all types of boundaries. How the hell would they be able to come back from that?

"Say somethin'," Eli said.

"Can you please let me go?" Kylee said calmly.

"You gon' chill wit' hittin' me?"

"Yeah, I'ma chill. I'm not gon' hit you no more, but tell ya bitch I'm maulin' her on sight," Kylee said, and meant every word. "So her best bet is to stay the fuck away from me!"

"You haven't calmed down," Eli said.

"I'm cool, I promise," she said calmly.

Eli was skeptical at first, but he went ahead and let go of Kylee's arms. Kylee did what she promised: she calmed down. She then turned and walked away.

"Where you goin'?" Eli asked.

"I don't know. This is too much," she said as she continued to cry. "I gotta get outta here and clear my head. When I get back I want you to be the fuck up outta my house!" Kylee grabbed her keys and headed out the door.

Shit had just gotten real. Eli stood in the middle of the living room feeling like shit. He loved Kylee with all his heart and there was no way he was leaving. He had lost and given up too much already; if he could forgive her, she was going to have to try to forgive him too. Knowing he had done the ultimate no-no, Eli started packing his belongings.

Chapter Twenty-seven

Kylee got in her car and tried calling Ja'Nay several times only to have her calls go straight to voicemail. Kylee was beyond heated as she started up her car and pulled off. She was on her way over to Ja'Nay's; there was no way she was about to let this ride. Pregnant or not, Kylee had planned on whoopin' Ja'Nay's ass for this one. She turned down Ja'Nay's street and stopped in front of the house. There wasn't a light on. Kylee sat in her car and waited for almost an hour to see if Ja'Nay would come home. Tired of waiting, Kylee pulled off and called I'reon.

"Naw, sis, tell me it ain't so?" I'reon said, shaking her head in disgust.

"I wish I could." Kylee bawled. Every time she thought about Ja'Nay being pregnant by Eli it made her cry.

"How long you think they have been messin' around?" I'reon asked.

"I don't know. He said it only happened once," Kylee said, wiping the snot and tears away from her face.

"Wow! Do you believe him?" I'reon asked.

"I don't know what to believe anymore," Kylee said.

"Where you at?" I'reon asked, knowing Kylee she was at Ja'Nay's house.

"Just leavin' Ja'Nay's house," Kylee answered.

"I knew it." I'reon laughed. "Girl, stay the fuck away from that bitch. You know her scary ass ain't gon' fight you. She gon' fuck around and call the police on you."

Kylee knew I'reon was right. Ja'Nay wouldn't be pregnant forever. She would eventually get the chance to dig off up in her ass!

"Where Eli's ass at?" I'reon frowned.

"I left that bitch at the house. I told him I wanted him gone when I got back!"

"You think he gon' leave?" I'reon questioned.

"He don't have no choice but to get the fuck outta mines! His name ain't on shit!" Kylee fumed.

"Well wit' him bein' gone, how you gon' pay your bills?"

"I'll manage, like always," Kylee answered.

"Well you know if you ever need some money, I got you," I'reon said.

"Thanks, sis," Kylee said, grateful that she had at least one loyal friend.

"No need to thank me, that's what friends are for," I'reon said.

"Well, look, I'm about to let you go on back to sleep. I forgot y'all five hours ahead of us." Kylee laughed, thankful she had I'reon to help calm her down.

"All right, girl. And stay yo' ass away from Ja'Nay," I'reon warned.

"I will."

"Promise me!" I'reon demanded.

"I will, but only until after she has that baby; then I'ma put my foot off up in her ass!" Kylee said.

"That's wassup! All right, I love you."

"Love you too," Kylee said, hanging up and heading over to the one place she knew no matter what she'd always be welcome.

"Mom, you in here?" Kylee yelled, walking into her parents' house. Seeing their cars parked in the driveway, but getting no answer, Kylee walked down the hall and into her parents' room. "Mom, you in here?" Kylee asked again, pushing the bedroom door open. She saw her mom sitting on the bed, crying, with a black eye and busted lip.

"What the fuck happened to you?" Kylee screamed. Seeing her mother's face made her cry all over again. "Who did this to you?"

"Don't cry, I'm fine, Kylee," her mother assured her, but Kylee wasn't buying it.

"Did Daddy do this to you?"

Her mother didn't respond.

"Answer me dammit! Did that muthafucka do this to you?" Kylee screamed as tears streamed down her face. Kylee was furious.

Kylee's mother was in a fragile state. "Kylee, don't talk about your father like that! All your life the only thing he tried to do was protect you," her mother cried.

"Fuck that! How you gon' let that nigga put his hands on you? I've always despised you for lettin' that nigga dog you the way that he does! You've always taught me to dog a nigga before he ever gets the chance to dog me! So much for takin' your own advice!" Kylee screamed as tears rolled down her cheeks.

"Because I deserve it, that's why I let him treat me like shit!" her mother screamed as the tears flowed.

"Mom, what you sayin' don't make sense! No woman deserves to get beat," Kylee frowned.

"I do, Kylee," her mother said as guilt ate away at her. "Because he knows he's not your real father," her mother blurted out.

Kylee froze while thinking she was hearing things. "What are you talkin' about, Mommy?"

"Look, Kylee you are not a little girl anymore and deserve to know the truth!" her mother stated sternly.

"The truth about what?" Kylee asked, confused.

"I had an affair years ago and your father found out about it. We were young and really didn't know what we wanted at the time. He was doin' his dirt, messin' around wit' Sylvia and other women."

Kylee was outdone that her mother knew about her dad's ongoing affair with Sylvia. She was even more surprised that her mother was having an affair as well. "During one of the times we broke up, I ended up gettin' pregnant by the guy I was messin' around with."

Kylee sat in silence as tears streamed down her face while her mother spoke. She was in complete awe.

"But your father and I decided to stay together and work on our marriage, because we thought we loved each other. He agreed to raise you as his own child, but over the years your father has never been able to get over the fact that you aren't biologically his. It has nothin' to do with you, because in his eyes, you are his child; he just can't forgive me."

Kylee was at a loss for words. She could not believe what her mother was telling her.

"He wanted to tell you a long time ago, but I refused to let him. That's why he used to lash out at me all the time. He was feelin' guilty for lyin' to you and felt you had the right to know. He used to take his anger out on me because I didn't want him to tell you."

Kylee wanted to ask questions but didn't know what to ask. Her mind was clouded with all kinds of thoughts. All these years the man she called and thought was her daddy wasn't. Kylee knew after that night her life would never be the same. She didn't know if it would make her better or bitter. Kylee built up enough nerve to ask her mother the one question she should have been expecting.

"Who is my real dad then?" Kylee finally asked.

Her mother looked at her as tears rolled down her face and said, "Tony."

Before Kylee could respond, her father walked in the room and noticed the perplexed look on Kylee's face.

"I told her, Vince," her mother said crying.

"Kylee, I'm sorry, I've been wantin' to tell you ever since you were a little girl," her father explained frantically.

Kylee was mortified. She couldn't believe she'd been fuckin' her own father. Where they do that at?

"Who all knew?" Kylee cried, while thinking that's why she and I'reon resembled each other so much.

"Kylee, calm down, baby," her father said.

"Who all knew that Tony was my real dad?" she screamed.

"Everybody except you and Tony," her mother replied, wiping away her tears.

"Even I'reon?" Kylee asked, hoping the answer would be no.

"Even I'reon," her father cried.

Kylee couldn't believe she'd been betrayed by everybody who had claimed to love her. In her eyes all her relationships were built on lies and deceit.

She looked at her mom and dad with pure disgust and said harshly, "I know I can try to forgive you guys for this one day, but I really can't imagine when. The only feelin's I have for you two right now is hate!"

The words stung the both of them deep.

"Don't talk to us like that, Kylee. We're your parents," her father pleaded.

"You ain't none of my daddy," she said before turning to walk away.

Her parents stood in the middle of their bedroom and for the first time in years they held each other and cried.

Kylee cried as she walked down the hall. She entered the living room, looked at the big ten-by-thirteen family portrait of her, her mom, and dad, and knocked it off the wall. She watched as the glass shattered all over the floor before walking out the door, vowing never to speak to Vince and her mother again.

Chapter Twenty-eight

Kylee jumped in her car and drove off with no destination in mind. She couldn't explain the way she was feeling after finding out that Tony was her biological father. She was in shock, distressed, disgusted and outraged, and embarrassed just to name a few. How could she ever face him again knowing the truth? Thoughts of committing suicide ran through her mind, but she decided against it; she was too afraid to die. She felt completely alone. Of all the people in the world, she would have never thought I'reon would ever keep anything from her. Hurt and angry Kylee decided to cut her off too, right along with everyone else who had betrayed her. Kylee drove crying and thinking back on her life and all the mistakes she'd made; she racked her mind for clues to try and help make sense of things. The remark Sylvia had made the night of Tony's BBQ hit her like a ton of bricks. Needing answers, Kylee busted a U-turn and headed over to Tony's.

Fifteen minutes later, Kylee pulled up in Tony's driveway. She got out of the car, walked up to the door and rang the doorbell. Kylee waited impatiently for Marta to open the door.

"*Hola, Señorita* Kylee," Marta said, answering the door.

"Is Sylvia here?" Kylee asked, cutting to the chase.

Marta nodded her head yes, stood to the side, and waited for Kylee to walk in.

"Who is it, Marta?" Sylvia walked into the huge foyer and asked.

"Me," Kylee replied with a mug on her face.

"What do you want? Tony ain't here!" Sylvia frowned and turned to walk away.

"I'm not here for Tony, I'm here for you," Kylee snapped.

Sylvia stopped in her tracks and turned back around. "What you want from me? I don't have shit to offer you!" Sylvia snapped back.

"Yeah, you do. You got a muthafuckin' explanation and some answers," Kylee said angrily.

"What you want me to explain? The reason why you fuckin' my husband and gettin' paid swell to do so? If so, the only answer I have for that is you're a thirsty-ass ho!"

"And you not? Your slate ain't so squeaky clean, Sylvia. You fuckin' my dad remember,"

Kylee reminded her. "So you a little thirsty too. Only thing is, I was gettin' paid to obey my thirst, and all you was gettin' was a wet ass!"

"You just don't get it do you?" Sylvia said, shaking her head.

"Fuck all that! How come you didn't tell me Tony was my real dad?" Kylee yelled while walking toward Syliva. Her first thought was to whoop her ass, but she knew if she did that she wouldn't get the answers she came for.

"Oh, so you finally found out?" Sylvia asked with a sly grin. "And it wasn't my place to tell you."

"What the fuck you mean it wasn't your place? You were the only one who knew we was fuckin'!" Kylee snapped off.

"When I tried to tell you, you was so busy tryin'a be cute and cocky, you wouldn't listen to me, remember? Where's all that attitude at now?" Sylvia asked with a smirk.

"You never tried to tell me shit, Sylvia! You was playin' word games, dumb-ass ho," Kylee yelled.

Deep down Sylvia knew that remark was true.

"You a foul bitch and you gon' rot in hell for this one! How could you let me sleep wit' my dad?" Kylee asked, not being able to hold back the tears any longer. The thought of sleeping with Tony made her skin crawl.

"Well at least I'll have you and Tony there to keep me company," Sylvia spat.

"I'm so outdone wit' you," Kylee said, shaking her head in disgust.

"Did you forget you was fuckin' my husband? And you have the nerve to wonder why! Puhleeze," Sylvia hissed while rolling her eyes.

Kylee stood staring at Sylvia as she continued talking.

"You and Tony played yourselves. I just sat back and watched it unfold. So don't blame me. Yes, I coulda told y'all, but tell for what? I knew eventually you muthafuckas would get what y'all deserved," Sylvia replied vengefully.

"Oh, my goodness, how could anyone be so cruel and vindictive?" Kylee cried.

"Cruel and vindictive is when you daughter's fourteen-year-old friend is fuckin' your husband!" Sylvia snapped. "I sat up and cried many nights after I found out Tony was fuckin' you! Not just because he was messin' around on me, 'cause he's been doin' that our entire marriage, but because he was sleepin' wit' his own daughter and I knew the truth." Tears began to well in Sylvia's eyes as well but she refused to let them fall; at least not in front of Kylee.

"Well how come you didn't at least tell him?" Kylee asked.

"Tell him for what? I tried to tell my husband a long time ago to watch out for you hoes, 'cause y'all only want him for his money, but he wouldn't listen, so I let him fall on his fat-ass face." Sylvia laughed.

"But he's your husband," Kylee said, not believing what was what's coming out of Sylvia's mouth.

"I fell outta love wit'*my* husband years ago. The only reason I stuck around is for the money and the status. If it wasn't for that I'da been gone years ago. Plus, his sex game is garbage. I'm sure you know what I'm talkin' about." Sylvia smirked.

Kylee stood in the middle of the foyer crying. She was trying to stomach everything Sylvia was saying.

"Look at you standin' here, lookin' pathetic as shit! You want somebody to feel sorry for you, don't you? Well I don't!" Sylvia spat harshly.

For the first time ever, Kylee stood silently as the tears continuously rolled down her face and Sylvia continued assassinating her character.

"See what tryin'a be slick get you? Nothin'!"

Still standing there thinking back on all of the freaky things she and Tony had done together literally made Kylee sick.

"Hoes like you will fuck anything that moves. But like I told my husband years ago, money brings you the woman you want, struggles brings you the women you need." Sylvia chuckled.

"You a dirty bitch," Kylee said, not being able to hold her anger in any longer.

"Look, I'm about to go to bed. You can finish tellin' your problems on somebody else's sofa. Go get the answers from your lyin'-ass mama," Sylvia spat.

Sylvia had struck a nerve; even though Kylee wasn't fuckin' with her mother anymore, she wasn't about to let this conniving, foul-ass bitch talk about her. Without Sylvia seeing it coming, Kylee slapped the cowboy shit out of Sylvia, taking her off-guard.

"Bitch, if you ever try to dog my mom again, I will kill you!" Kylee said venomously.

Sylvia was stunned. She saw the look in Kylee's eyes and knew she better not open her mouth.

"One more thing, bitch: you weak," Kylee said, spitting in Sylvia's face before turning to walk away. Kylee looked over at Marta, who stood in the doorway of the living room, smiling, and continued out the door.

Kylee couldn't believe how her entire life had fallen apart in just one day, as she got in her car and sped off.

Kylee was bawling as she pulled up into her driveway. Her heart dropped when she noticed Eli's car was gone. She remembered she had told him to be gone when she got back. She had absolutely nobody to turn to now. Kylee got out of the car and looked over at Mr. Vernon's old place before walking into the house. She glanced down and noticed all Eli's shoes were gone from the foyer. She locked the door behind her and headed upstairs to her room. She looked around the room noticing all Eli's belongings were gone from there, too. She couldn't believe he had really left.

She didn't know what her next move would be. All she knew was it was her against the world. Kylee felt suffocated. Thoughts of the day's events continuously played in her head. She pulled her knees up to her chest and lay there until she drifted off to sleep.

Kylee jumped as she felt a hand on her arm. She turned around and looked up. She felt an enormous sense of relief seeing Eli standing there, looking down at her.

"Look, ma, I know I fucked up and it might take me a lifetime to make it right, but I'm willin' to stick around that long until I get it right, if you let me," Eli started.

Exchanging no words, Kylee sat up and listened to Eli pour out his heart.

Eli's eyes filled up with tears. "I don't know what it means to you when I say I love you, but it means everything to me to be able to show you and tell you. Kylee, I love you and I want you to be my wife. I know its gon' take time for us to get back where we were, but I'm willin' to work for it. I'm not lettin' you go. All you gotta do is tell me what I can do to make it right and I swear to you, I will make it happen." Eli sat down next to Kylee, wiped the tears away from her eyes, and waited for her to speak.

"Get me the fuck away from here!" Kylee cried.

Eli wrapped his strong arms around Kylee and pulled her into his chest as she cried.

"Just take me away from here, please," she begged as she wailed.

Eli knew there was a lot behind Kylee's pain. He could sense there was more going on than just him getting Ja'Nay pregnant. Kylee was releasing her pain through her tears. He was just glad she was willing to let him be the shoulder she needed to cry on. Eli meant every word he said about making things right between them. He loved Kylee and wasn't about to let nothing else ruin his chances of being happy, for the first time in his life.

Epilogue

Two Years Later

Kylee sat out on her front porch, smiling, while looking out at the beautiful, clear blue water as Eli ran around the yard playing with his two daughters.

"Be careful, nigga, those are not boys," Kylee yelled as Eli grabbed both girls in his arms and began swinging them around.

"I got this." He smiled as both girls giggled.

"I'm glad Tionna let you bring Sy'onn over here," Kylee looked over at Ja'Nay and said.

"I'm glad too. She was bein' a bitch at first until Big Ness told her it would be fucked up if she didn't let his daughter be a part of her daddy's weddin'. I guess she started feelin' bad and told me I could bring her wit' me."

"Yeah, man, that bitch do be trippin'. Eli told me when he first asked her, Edna's miserable ass was in the background talkin' shit about Sy'onn flyin' to Jamaica wit' a stranger," Kylee said, shaking her head.

"Fuck Edna." Ja'Nay laughed.

"That's what I said." Kylee laughed too.

"So, are you excited about the weddin'?" Ja'Nay asked, smiling, happy for her girl.

"I'm kinda' nervous." Kylee smiled.

"Don't be, girl; you gon' be a beautiful bride and I know Eli is gon' be a wonderful husband. I'm so glad you finally found happiness. I remember when you used to be dead set against fallin' in love," Ja'Nay said.

"Thanks, Ja'Nay. I really appreciate you flyin' over here to be a part of my weddin'," Kylee said gratefully. "Eli's family is being very helpful and supportive, but ain't nothin' like ya own."

"I wouldn't have missed this for the world. We been talkin' about bein' in each other's weddin's since I was gon' marry Michael Jackson during his *Thriller* days and you was gon' marry Prince during his *Purple Rain* days," Ja'Nay said, laughing.

"Right." Kylee laughed too forgetting all about their schoolgirl crushes.

"Are you gon' invite I'reon and your parents?" Ja'Nay asked carefully.

Kylee thought for a brief moment before answering. "I haven't spoken to them since I left Ohio. It's been two years so I doubt if they would even come."

"You never know."

"You right, I won't," Kylee said sadly.

"Kylee, don't be like that," Ja'Nay pleaded.

"Whatever," Kylee said, waving Ja'Nay off. "You just don't know."

"I know yo' daddy would love to walk his only daughter down the aisle," Ja'Nay said, smiling.

When Kylee was a little girl she had dreamt of having Vince give her away to whatever special man was lucky enough to become her husband. Knowing that she had been lied to and deceived for so many years by her parents made it hard for her to face them much less have them present on her special day.

"I can't believe you didn't come home when Tony died," Ja'Nay said. "I just knew you would be there front and center. You loved your godfather."

A little too much, Kylee thought.

Thinking and talking about Tony still stirred up sad feelings inside of Kylee. Even though she never got to speak to him before he passed, she still had a soft spot in her heart for him; he was her biological father.

"I didn't wanna be around all them fake muthafuckas! So I just sent flowers. That was enough," Kylee said, wanting to be there but unable to face her past.

"Man, that funeral was packed like a Lil Wayne concert," Ja'Nay joked.

"I bet it was," Kylee said, smiling.

"I feel so sorry for I'reon though," Ja'Nay said.

"What's wrong wit' her?" Kylee inquired.

"Man, after Tony died, she just been depressed and shit. Every time I call her she in the bed, 'sleep. Even wit' all the money and other shit Tony left her and this sister no one knew about, she still goin' through it."

"Sister?" Kylee asked. *Damn, I thought me and I'reon were his only kids.*

"Yeah, word on the street is Tony had another daughter no one knew about and he left her half his money, some property, and some other stuff. I heard she didn't want anything to do wit' Tony; that's why she never contacted his estate attorney to claim her possessions," Ja'Nay said, repeating the rumors that were going around.

"Damn, Tony got another daughter? That's crazy," Kylee said.

"Oooooh, and I heard he didn't leave Sylvia shit! I guess she'd been messin' around on him and Tony knew about it but never said anything, and when she went to the readin' of the will, he left her absolutely nothin'. She had to move out the house and everything," Ja'Nay said.

Karma, Kylee thought with a smile. "Sylvia was messin' around? Wow, that's crazy. Did anyone know who with?" Kylee asked.

"Naw, the streets ain't singin' no names, and yeah, that's messed up she was cheatin' all the time," Ja'Nay said, shaking her head in disbelief.

"So, have you heard from Quann lately?" Kylee asked, changing the subject.

"Yeah, he called me the other day and asked me if I could send him a food box," Ja'Nay replied.

"That nigga still in jail?" Kylee asked, surprised.

"Yeah, he got out and went right back like thirty days later. This time he gon' be gone for about ten years," Ja'Nay said uncaringly.

"So what you tell him about the food box?"

"I told him hell naw! I got a child to take care of now and if he woulda treated me like I deserved to be treated while he was out, I wouldn'a minded holdin' him down while he locked up! He betta get one of them other bitches to get him a box. I'm done bein' his dummy." Ja'Nay frowned.

"I heard that." Kylee smiled, happy that her girl had finally come to her senses.

"I need to take this; this Tay," Ja'Nay said, looking down at her ringing cell phone.

"Ummm, he callin' to check on his woman." Kylee laughed.

"Whatever." Ja'Nay laughed before standing up and walking into the house to answer her call. Kylee looked out at the girls as they had fun with their dad and smiled. She loved the fact Eli was a stand-up father when it came to his children. They wanted for nothing. At first, Kylee selfishly told Eli she wanted him to have nothing to do with Ja'Nay and their daughter. After the birth of Reign and the DNA coming back 99.9 percent positive that Eli was the father, Kylee knew it wasn't right for Eli to not be a part of his daughter's life.

Kylee continued watching Eli play with the girls. She knew she'd made the right choice by leaving the country with the man she loved. Eli made her happier than she'd ever been. She was more than grateful that he'd done everything he promised her he'd do. He made sure that every day of her life was spent happy. No doubt they had their ups and downs like any other relationship, but Eli went out of his way to make sure there were more ups than anything. For the past year he'd even tried to repair her broken relationship with I'reon and her parents. Being the stubborn person she was she always refused to do so. Eli still never knew the real reason behind their fallout, but he always stressed to her that whatever happened it couldn't be that bad to where they couldn't work it out. True enough, Kylee wanted to call her parents, but she didn't know how they would react toward her. After Tony had died from a heart attack the urge had become stronger, because even though she hadn't talked to them, the thought of losing them would still be too much for her to bear.

Tears filled Kylee's eyes as thoughts of parents and not having the opportunity to say good-bye crossed her mind. She'd forgiven people for doing way worse; why not her own parents? In the end they were only trying to protect her, and Vince had never treated her any differently. It wasn't their fault she'd been sleeping with her own dad, which was really the root of all her pain and turmoil. Kylee had felt so low and dirty she was unable to admit any blame in the situation that had been created.

Eli walked up on the porch and leaned down and gave Kylee a kiss on the lips.

"What was that for?" she looked up and asked, smiling.

"Just because I love you," Eli said, smiling back.

"I love you too, Eli, more than you will ever know."

"Trust me, I know." He winked before walking back off the porch and continued playing with the girls.

Kylee was satisfied with her life, but it still wasn't complete. Even with a fiancé who loved her to death, a beautiful home, and her best friend back, something was still missing. She pulled out her cell phone and dialed her parents' home phone. Her heart pounded as she waited on one of them to answer.

"Hello?" they both answered at the same time.

"Mommy, Daddy?" Kylee said as tears formed in her eyes.

"Kylee?" they both asked, shocked. They were hoping this wasn't a cruel trick; it had been so long since they had heard from their daughter.

"Yes," Kylee said as the tears fell.

"Oh, my God, Vince, it's our baby," her mother cried.

Hearing her mother still consider her their baby brought a smile to her face. "I love y'all," Kylee cried.

"We love you too, Kylee," they said simultaneously.

After speaking to her parents and them agreeing to fly in so Vince, her daddy, could walk his baby girl down the aisle, Kylee was ecstatic. She hung up with her parents and knew what she had to do in order for her life to be complete: she called I'reon.

"Hello?" I'reon answered.

"I'reon?"

"Yes?"

"This Kylee."

I'reon was quiet at first. Kylee thought that was a bad sign.

"Look, I know you probably mad at me but I'm sorry," Kylee said.

"Bitch, 'bout time you called me. I've been waitin' to hear from you for two years," I'reon said happily.

Kylee was relieved. "I'm sorry, I was just goin' through some things and I just wanna apologize."

"Look, girl, I understand and I'm the one who owes you an apology," I'reon said.

"What you do?" Kylee inquired.

"I had no business keepin' a secret like that from you, but I promised my mom I wouldn't say anything to you. I used to feel bad because I couldn't tell you." I'reon's eyes filled with tears. "And I found out after dad had passed that y'all was messin' around."

"I don't wanna talk about that," Kylee said, feeling sick to her stomach.

"I know, Kylee, that it's a touchy subject, but I promised myself that if I ever got the chance to speak to you I would tell you this."

"What?" Kylee asked quickly.

"Dad knew you was his daughter," I'reon said.

"What?" Kylee asked, not believing what I'reon was telling her.

"Yeah, he knew. Before he died he had wrote me a letter tellin' me that you was his daughter and he was sleepin' with you. He didn't know at first, he found out by mistake, but it was too late so he continued sleeping with you 'cause he didn't look at you like his daughter. That's why he gave you a monthly allowance, trying to compensate for knowin' he was fuckin' his own daughter," I'reon said, shaking her head in disgust.

Kylee was in awe hearing Tony knew she was his child. Kylee was done crying; that was all in her past. She was about to take the same advice she had once given to Tionna and many other females. She was about to focus on her future and forget her past and move on.

"So, I hear Tony had another daughter he left money to but she didn't want it," Kylee said, upset because he'd left her with nothing but ill feelings.

"That's only because they couldn't find her," I'reon said.

"Well where is she?"

"Over in Jamaica," I'reon said, smiling.

"What's her name? Maybe I can help you find her," Kylee said.

"She's not lost. I'm talkin' to her ass right now," I'reon said, laughing.

"Who me?" Kylee asked, surprised.

"Yeah, you. Me and you were his only children," I'reon said, laughing. "Nobody knew where you were at so your money is just sittin' in a trust fund."

"Wow, how much is it?" Kylee asked, happy.

"Let's just say you'll never have to work another day in your life, not that you planned on gettin' a job anyways," I'reon joked.

"You're right about that." Kylee laughed.

"It sure is nice hearin' from you, sis."

Even though I'reon had called Kylee sis for years, saying the word now and knowing that they really were sisters gave the word a different feeling. "I feel the same way," Kylee said, glad that I'reon wasn't mad at her for cutting her out of her life for the last two years.

Kylee and I'reon talked a few more minutes. She was happy when I'reon agreed to take the next flight out to be a part of her wedding. Kylee was even happier when I'reon said Shawn wouldn't be able to come on such short notice. Kylee didn't know how to tell her sister that Eli and his family weren't big on gays anyways. After she hung up, Ja'Nay walked back out on the porch with a huge smile on her face.

"What you smilin' for?" Kylee looked up at her and asked.

"I'm just happy that's all. I got my best friend back, I got my baby, my man, and I'm just in a happy place in my life right now."

"That's wassup." Kylee smiled, genuinely happy for her girl.

"I just wish I'reon could be here to share our happiness," Ja'Nay said.

"Your wish will be granted 'cause her and my parents are flyin' out tonight." Kylee smiled.

"For real?" Ja'Nay asked, skeptically.

"Yeah, I'm for real." Kylee smiled.

"When did you talk to 'em?"

"When you were in the house talkin' to Tay," Kylee answered.

"That's what I'm talkin' about," Ja'Nay said happily. "This is the best day of my life."

"Mines too," Kylee agreed.

"What made you change your mind about callin' 'em?"

Kylee looked over at Ja'Nay before she spoke. "It was just time," was all Kylee said.

Ja'Nay smiled and shook her head in agreement.

Kylee looked over at Ja'Nay and smiled. She was happy to have her girl back in her life. It had taken time, but Ja'Nay and Kylee had rebuilt their relationship. It took Kylee time to realize, understand, and feel all the pain and destruction she'd caused on other relationships, including Tionna's and Sylvia's. Ja'Nay had been trying to tell her for so long that eventually karma would make *her* way back around, and without it being planned Ja'Nay ended up being the one teaching Kylee firsthand how it felt. How could she not forgive Ja'Nay for making a mistake when for years she'd been the sneaky, devious chick who men loved only because she'd been willing to do what ya girl won't do!